The Dark Alley

The Dark Alley

ASHOK SRIDHARAN

PARTRIDGE

A Penguin Random House Company

ISBN:	Softcover	978-1-4828-3555-7
	eBook	978-1-4828-3553-3

To order additional copies of this book, contact
Partridge India
000 800 10062 62
orders.india@partridgepublishing.com

www.partridgepublishing.com/india

Contents

To Jayasri, my friend, companion, guide and my inspiration

A Blind Case

It was around half past six in the evening. ACP Hrishikesh Bharadwaj was seated in his cabin. A giant of a man, there was a look of intensity in his eyes which bespoke an iron will. Now in his mid 30s, Hrishi was regarded as one of the most promising young officers in the state IPS cadre.

He was sipping from the glass of water on his desk when the phone started ringing. "Hello?" said he, picking up the receiver.

"Hello Bharadwaj, DCP Patkar here. Can you come upstairs?"

"Yes Sir. Just a minute," said Hrishi. He got up and rushed to DCP Patkar's cabin on the second floor. He had met him just once before for little more than a formal introduction. This was to be Hrishi's first proper meeting with the new DCP.

It was just two days since DCP Shrikant Patkar had taken charge of the recently constituted Madhavgadh Crime Branch, which was responsible for the entire district. The newly elected government had launched a crusade to improve the deteriorating law and order situation in the state. Consequently Shrikant had been pulled out of his existing posting and transferred to the second biggest city in the state. Hrishi, who had himself been transferred to Madhavgadh less than a month ago, owed his presence there to the recent restructuring.

He was immediately ushered into the cabin of DCP Patkar. Shrikant was a slightly built man with a benign look. He looked a college professor rather than a policeman. Many had made the

1

fatal error of underestimating him, only to realise that there lurked beneath those benign features a tough, ruthless man. Shrikant looked nearer fifty, although he was not yet his mid 40s - the legacy of a two year punishment posting in naxal infested territory after he had arrested the son of an MLA.

"*Aao bhai Bharadwaj. Baitho,*" said Shrikant, motioning Hrishi to be seated.

"*Ji Sir,*" said Hrishi, taking his seat.

"*Chai peoge?*"

"No, thank you Sir."

"*Sharmao mat bhai.* No formalities with me," said Shrikant, much to the astonishment of Hrishi, who was used to overbearing and at times even arrogant officers.

"Okay Sir," said Hrishi.

"Perfect! *Yeh hui na baat.*" Shrikant called for two cups of tea.

"Well Bharadwaj, I want you to take charge of a murder case that's been transferred to us," said Shrikant, having got over the pleasantries. "The body was found by the river bank at Kanheda on the 25th of last month with deep stab wounds. The local police there has made no progress, which is why the case has been transfered here."

"Why us Sir? I mean, Kanheda is so far from here."

"There are no crime branch officers there. Since Kanheda is in our district, the case automatically came to us," replied Shrikant.

"I see," said Hrishi. With the existing workload, a case from Kanheda was the last thing he needed.

"The body has not been identified. No documents were found on the corpse. Here's the file. I fear we don't have too many details here."

"Alright."

"I know its not easy Bharadwaj. You're searching a needle in a haystack, but you'll have to make the best of what's available. I've heard a lot about you, which is why I'm giving you this case."

"Thank you Sir," said Hrishi. "I'll give it my best."

"I understand that you're on the Dhanraj murder case. That case assumes first priority. Delegate this to one of your officers. Just take charge of this."

"No problem Sir," said Hrishi.

He cursed under his breath. Why on earth was the responsibility of the biggest district in the state thrust upon a single, chronically understaffed department?

The Investigation Begins

Hrishi came rushing to his table, where Inspector Manish Deshpande was waiting for him. Manish was nearing thirty, although he looked much younger with his boyish features.

"Yes Manish, what's the matter?"

"Sir its regarding the body that was found at Kanheda last month."

"Okay. Any update on that case?"

"Sir I went to Kanheda yesterday. I checked out the site where the body was found. I've also collected all the evidence that the local police collected."

"Okay. What did you get?"

"Nothing at the site Sir. Its been more than a month since the body was found there. With all the rains we've had, whatever marks could have been there have been wiped out."

"What about photographs of the site where the body was found?"

"None at all Sir. No such arrangement was made."

"Okay. Were there any documents on the dead man?"

"No Sir. his pockets were clean. There was no mobile phone either."

"I see. So the body has not yet been identified I guess."

"Yes Sir. They circulated the photographs among their informers and released ads in the local newspapers. The only response they got was from a panwallah who remembered seeing him and two of the operators at the toll gate outside Kanheda. They had seen him several times, but none of them knew who the man was."

"Did you meet them?"

"I did Sir, but that was about all that I got from them. One of those fellows at the toll naka told me that this man went past the toll gate on 24th July, the day before the body was found."

"Was he sure of the date?"

"Actually he couldn't remember the date, but he remembered that it was about a month ago and it was the day on which it rained very heavily. They had over 100 mm of rain that day, which is a record for Kanheda. So there's no doubt about the date."

"Okay. What time did that fellow go past the toll naka?"

"It was in the evening Sir. Sometime after seven."

"Alright. If this fellow went past the toll gate, its obvious that he had a car. Any idea about the model or registration number?"

"It was a Tata Safari Sir. Registration number unknown."

"*Chalo, bhagte chor ki langoti hi sahi.* We at least have our first clue. We can start off assuming that the car was his and that its registered in our state."

"There will be several thousand Sir."

"I know Manish, but it isn't as if we're spoilt for options. Anyway, what else do we have"

"There's the photograph Sir. The face was slightly disfigured, but still recognisable look," said Manish, handing over the available photographs to Hrishi.

"Good, so we have a face too. What else?"

"Nothing much Sir. The man was about 5'9", wheatish complexion. He was of average built."

"Half the men in this state will fit that description. What about the body?"

"Its already been disposed off Sir. The hospital morgue had limited storage space. They couldn't preserve the body indefinitely."

"Which means there's nothing more to fall back. What about the autopsy?" asked Hrishi.

"Here it is Sir."

Hrishi browsed through the contents. The dead man was between 33 and 36 years of age. From the timing of the post mortem, it was evident that the death had occured between 7 and 10 P.M on 24th July. The cause of death was drowning. The doctor had added a note that there was heavy blood loss due to the stab wounds, which could have caused death even if the victim had not drowned.

"So there's no doubt that its a case of murder. The guy who did it got rid of anything that could have helped us identify the corpse. What about the clothes that he was wearing?

"Nothing much in it Sir," replied Manish, pulling the evidence bag which he had kept in the chair next to his.

Hrishi pulled them out of the holder spread them out on the table. The man wore a white *ganjee* and navy-blue trousers.

"The shirt is missing for whatever reason. The trousers are readymade. I don't see any laundry marks either. *Hathyaare ne badi safai se kaam kiya.* He's pretty much wiped out all traces," said Hrishi. Manish nodded.

"As I see it, there's only one way out. Get the list of Tata Safaris registered in this state. That should narrow the field out to a few hundred. Also get in touch with all police stations in the state and get the list of missing persons. Someone must have surely filed a missing complaint."

"Sure Sir," replied Manish.

"I know its going to take time and I fully understand that this is far too much work for one person to handle. Take Mane and Sharma. I'll release them from all existing cases for the next two days. Put your best foot forward boss."

"Sure Sir."

Identification

Manish knocked the door of Hrishi's cabin. "Come in," came the familiar voice. Manish entered the cabin.

"Oh Manish, *aao bhai. Baith jao.*"

"Thank you Sir, I came to update you about the Kanheda murder case."

"Okay, got something new?"

"Sir I believe we have identified the dead man. There's a man called Nilesh Karhadkar who happens to own a Safari registered in Shilahar. He also appears on the missing persons list. Look."

Hrishi looked at the missing person complaint lodged at Gandhi Nagar police station in Shilahar. It was lodged on 25th July by a lady called Priya Karhadkar, the missing man's wife. Priya's husband Nilesh had gone to meet a friend in Kanheda on 23rd July and was supposed to return the following evening, but never turned up.

"The photographs look the same. Yes boss, this is our man! Call Priya Karhadkar. Ask her to come here."

Priya Karhadkar was seated with another man in Hrishi's cabin, where Manish and ASI Asha Kadam too were present. Priya had only just entered and introduced herself.

"Good morning Priyaji. And good morning to you too Mr..." said Hrishi, turning to the man seated next to her. He was in his late thirties, with a noticeable paunch and an expression that bespoke a suspicious nature.

"I'm Pravin Patel Sir. Nilesh and I are partners and I'm also a family friend," replied the man.

"Sir please let me know what happened to Nilesh? Have you found him?" asked Priya.

"Just a minute Priyaji. Manish, could you please speak to Mr. Pravin?"

"Sure Sir. Come with me Pravin saahab," said Manish, motioning him to follow.

"I..."

"We need to speak to Priyaji in private Mr. Pravin. Please go with Inspector Deshpande," said Hrishi in a tone that sounded more like an order than a request.

"Okay Sir."

Hrishi took out the photograph of the dead man the moment Pravin left. "Do you recognise the man in this picture Priyaji?" asked Hrishi, handing her the photograph.

There was a look of horror mingled with dismay on Priya's face as she saw the picture. "That's my husband Sir, what happened to him?"

"I fear the news isn't good Priyaji. He was found dead in Kanheda on the 25th of last month," said Hrishi, rather reluctantly.

"My God! How?"

"He died of drowning, though we have every reason to believe he was murdered," replied Hrishi, prefering not to dwell on the details.

"I can't believe it," said Priya, shaking her head is disbelief.

Hrishi turned to Asha and nodded. She got the message.

"I can understand your shock Priyaji. I *er...* I know this is not the right time, but...I need to ask you a few questions," said Asha, taking over.

Priya Karhadkar nodded.

"When did you last see your husband?"

"23rd July. He had gone to Kanheda for a reunion with some of his school friends. He was to come back on the 24th, but he never returned."

"I see. What time did he leave on the 23rd?"

"He left from his office that afternoon, I'm not sure of the timing."

"How did he go there?"

"He drove down. Nilesh loves driving."

"Okay. So if I understand correctly, it was a boy's reunion," said Asha. Priya nodded. "Do you know the names of the friends he was supposed to meet?"

"Nilesh mentioned someone called Ravi Dixit. I'm not sure who the others were."

"Do you have their numbers?"

Priya Karhadkar shook her head.

"What about the car? I understand Nilesh had a Tata Safari."

"Yes Ma'am. Nilesh never returned, nor did his car."

Asha turned to Hrishi, who nodded. Here was the second clue. "Could you give me the registration and engine chasis number?" asked she.

"I remember the registration number, but I don't know the chasis number."

"In that case we'll need to get all documents relating to the car Priyaji. The chasis number will definitely be mentioned somewhere. Please fax it to us once you get them. The car could be an important lead," said Asha. Priya nodded.

"So what happened Priyaji? You said that your husband left on the 23rd. What happened then?"

"Nilesh called me up to say that he had reached and all was fine. He even called me around seven in the evening of the 24th to say that he was leaving. Kanheda is about one and a half to two hours from

9

where we live, so he should have reached by nine at the outermost. I started getting anxious by nine thirty, so I called, but his mobile was switched off. I tried repeatedly, but everytime I got the same response."

"Okay, what did you do then?"

"I called up Pravin to find out whether he had any knowledge of Nilesh's whereabouts."

"I see. So is Pravin a close friend of Nilesh?"

"Yes Ma'am. We know each other since a long time now. We grew up in Shastri Nagar in Pune. We know each other since our school days, so our association goes a long way back."

"Pravin mentioned that he and Nilesh are partners. So they have a business or something like that?"

"That's right. They are both Chartered Accountants. They have been in practice since four years now."

"Okay. Now let's go back to the night of 24th July. You said that you called Pravin. What time was it?"

"That must have been around eleven."

"Okay. What happened then?"

"He advised me to wait for a little longer. He came around midnight to inquire about Nilesh, but there was still no sign of him. I went to the police station the next morning to lodge a complaint. Since then, I've not heard anything until your officer called me up today morning."

"Okay... Like I said Priyaji, your husband was murdered. Do you suspect anyone? Any enemies or anyone with a grudge?"

Priya Karhadkar shook her head. "My husband was a perfectly normal and decent man. Why should anyone wish him any harm?"

"Is there any dispute? Property or money, or anything of the sort?"

"No Ma'am. Nilesh is from a middle class family. There's no land or any such property that someone could fight over. His brother lives in Canada and he's quite well off."

"I see," said Asha, turning to her officer.

"Thank you very much for your cooperation Priyaji. Please give us Nilesh's mobile number as well as the registration number of the car. And please fax us the documents relating to the car. We need the chasis number," said Hrishi.

"I'll get you the details Sir, but I need the body."

"Well I er... I'm sorry Priyaji, the body was destroyed. We have the ashes with us. ASI Asha will take you through the formalities," said Hrishi, nodding to Asha.

"Okay," said Priya.

—⋯⋯—

"What do you think?" asked Hrishi. Priya and Pravin had just left.

"*Daal mein kuch kala hai Sir*. I've been married since a dozen years now. She didn't look or sound like a woman who just heard about the death of her husband. You saw how she reacted when we told her that the body was destroyed? Just a simple 'okay'. You don't expect a woman who's lost her husband to be so cool."

"Agree with you, that looks rather fishy. I wonder... Let's have those guys in Shilahar keep an eye on her."

Just then Manish entered. "Hey Manish. What did you get?" asked Hrishi, wasting no time.

"Here's the statement Sir," said Manish, placing the register before his senior officer. "According to Pravin, Nilesh had gone to Kanheda for a reunion with his school friends on 23rd July. He was to return on the 24th, but never came back."

"Tallies with what Priya told us. Let's see the rest of it," said Hrishi. He browsed throught the contents of Manish's report. "Here, look. The other facts tally, but there's a slight difference here. Pravin says that they were from the same area, but he didn't really know her until Nilesh and she married, but Priya says that they know each other right from the time they were in Pune. *Kyon*?"

11

"*Gadbad hai Sir,*" said Manish.

"Well my dear fellow, now you know why I insist on our speaking to people seperately. Anyway, here's where it stands now: Nilesh Karhadkar was murdered on the night of 24th July and thrown into the river somewhere near Kanheda. Who did it and why he did it, we don't know yet. We first need to establish a motive."

"What about the car Sir? We could have a clue there. A car cannot just disappear."

"Yes Manish, we need to explore that angle too. We have the registration number. Once we get the engine chasis number, let's put all the police stations in the state on the alert. Secondly, get the complete phone records of Nilesh, Priya and Pravin. Put their numbers on tracking."

"But Sir, Nilesh's phone is switched off."

"Get the IMEI number Manish. Put that on tracking. That's the way forward as of now. In the meanwhile, I'll arrange to have Priya and Pravin shadowed by the guys in Shilahar. Let's see what we get there."

"Okay Sir."

"We also need to trace down this Dixit fellow who Nilesh went to meet. Ravi Dixit could throw some light on this puzzle. Either he or the others in that reunion should know a thing or two. Who knows, it could be something to do with an event from Nilesh's school or college days."

"Could be Sir."

"Look into it Manish. I'm tied up with the Dhanraj murder case, so I'll have to leave this to you."

"No problem Sir."

Following the Trail

Manish stepped into the room where his table was located. He was looking sweaty and weary. He had evidently had a tough day in the field. Constable Govind Mane was waiting for him.

"*Haan* Govind, why did you call me?" asked Manish, wasting no time.

"Sir we got a communication from St. Vincent's school in Pune. That's the one where Nilesh Karhadkar did his schooling."

"Okay. Any news on Ravi Dixit?"

"Yes Sir. There was a student called Ravi Dixit in the SSC batch of '94, the same year in which Nilesh completed his tenth."

"I see. Anything else?"

"No Sir, that's all," said Mane. "The address they gave is an old one. I know Pune well, my brother lives not very far from that area. There's a shopping mall in the place where this fellow's house used to be."

"Alright, have you got the photograph?"

"Ji Sir, there you are," said Mane.

"Thank you," said Manish. Mane was too old and too set in his ways to think beyond his instructions. Nonetheless, there was at least a photograph to work with, albeit one that was nearly twenty years old.

Manish logged into facebook and searched Nilesh Karhadkar. Within seconds he had opened Nilesh Karhadkar's friends list. He quickly scrolled through the names.

Ravi Dixit appeared on the list.

Manish took a quick glance at the photograph. It certainly was the same fellow. Despite the passage of years, the face was unmistakably the same, only a couple of decades older. Manish clicked on the link. Ravi Dixit worked for TCS now. No other details were available, but he had his lead now.

Manish dialled TCS' head office and asked for the HR department. He was transferred to a man called Najib Ali. "Hello Mr. Najib, I'm Inspector Manish Deshpande from Madhavgadh Crime Branch."

"Hello Sir, how can I help you?" asked Najib.

"Mr. Najib, I need information about an employee of yours called Ravi Dixit."

"Which branch Sir?

"I don't know Mr. Najib. The information I have, apart from the name, is that he did his schooling from St. Vincent's school in Pune. That's all I have. I can send you a photograph if needed."

"Please do that Sir, I'll fish out the details."

"Okay, give me your e-mail ID," said Manish. he quickly jotted down the address that Najib gave him.

Manish was at *a tapri* having a *samosa pao* that evening, when his mobile phone started ringing. "Hello?" said he, pressing the green button.

"Hello Sir, I'm Najib Ali from TCS."

"Yes Mr. Najib, tell me."

"Sir I managed to get the records relating to Ravi Dixit. Unfortunately he's no longer with TCS. He left last December."

"I see. Do you have his contact details?"

"No Sir. we don't have any information relating to him post last December. I can give you his personal email ID and mobile number. I don't know whether its still active, but you can take it down."

"Okay, tell me," said Manish. He jotted down both details. "Thank you very much Mr. Najib. Tell me, which branch was he posted in?"

"He was in our Baroda branch Sir."

"Okay, give me the name and contact number of his boss, if that person is still with you."

"No Sir, he too is gone. He was reporting to Sukumar Panikker, who passed away this April."

"I see. Too bad. Give me the number of the office where he worked. I'll get in touch with them," said Manish.

Manish dialled the mobile number that Najib had given him, but the number was no longer in existence. Manish shrugged his shoulders. He called up TCS' Baroda office, where he was presently transferred to a man called Deepak Malhotra. "Hello, Deepak Malhotra here," came the voice presently.

"Hello Deepak. I'm Inspector Manish Deshpande from Madhavgadh Crime Branch. I need to speak to you about a former employee of yours called Ravi Dixit."

"Ravi? What happened to him?"

"Nothing Mr. Malhotra. But I believe he could give us valuable information relating to an investigation. I have been trying to reach him on his personal mobile number, but the number is an old one. Would you know where I can reach him?"

"I have no idea officer. He got a job in Australia. He's been living there since last December."

"Australia! He's no longer in the country?"

"Yes Sir, I believe so. There's a guy here called Ramnath Subramaniam who could give me his details, Ram and Ravi were good friends. Unfortunately Ram is on holiday now and he's presently unreachable."

"Alright, no problem. I'll find out. Thank you very much," said Manish.

So Ravi Dixit was in Australia now. If that information was true, it was highly unlikely that he could have been involved in this affair.

But if he was in Australia, whom had Nilesh gone to meet? Had Priya Karhadkar lied to them, or was there something more to it?

The only person who could confirm it was Ravi himself. If he didn't have the number, he at least had his online ID. He would have to send a message to Ravi on facebook.

━━◆━━

Manish knocked the door of Hrishi's cabin, where he was ushered in immediately. Seeing Hrishi's hassled expression, he got to the point quickly.

"Sir, this is regarding the Kanheda murder case."

"Okay, any progress on it?"

"Quite a bit Sir. I managed to trace down Ravi Dixit, that fellow whom Nilesh is supposed to have gone to meet. I managed to get him on Facebook. He's replied to my message."

"I see! What did he say?"

"Sir Ravi Dixit has been in Australia since last December. He's not been to India anytime since then. He's not met Nilesh since several years now and they have only intermittently been in contact, largely through the odd exchange on facebook."

"I see. So Priya Karhadkar was lying... or was she?"

"It should be that way Sir."

"*Nai* Manish, not necessarily. Don't forget that she filed a missing person complaint with the police. Why would she provide false information, knowing fully well we might get to the bottom of it? Either she's cooked up a pretty well thought out conspiracy, or there's something more to it."

"Could be Sir. As you're aware, I'm in touch with Jagdish Gaikwad from Gandhi Nagar police station in Shilahar. His men seem to have done a pretty good job. We've got information about every movement of theirs."

"Okay, and?"

"Let's start off with our man Nilesh himself Sir. He was apparently a dishonest chap. The general view of that guy is that he would sign any document if you showed him the money. Someone even went to the extent of saying that he would have happily put his hands in the gutter if there was money to be had."

"I see."

"And he was a drunkard too."

"Drunkard? Did he get into any drunken brawls?"

"No Sir. Not that we're aware of. On the contrary, he was the one who used to get bashed, especially by his wife. They say that he frequently got it from her."

"So the relationship between them was not particularly great."

"Yes Sir. It looks like they stayed together only because of their son, who's now four."

"I see. That perhaps explains her reaction when she heard about his death."

"There's one more thing Sir. Apparently, Nilesh was Insured for eighty lakhs. The nominee was his wife Priya Karhadkar and she's already started the documentation process for staking a claim."

"I see! So Priya Karhadkar stood to gain quite handsomely from her husband's death. Hmm..."

"There's more to it Sir. Apparently Priya and Pravin have been meeting pretty much on a daily basis since Nilesh disappeared, which is about a month now."

"You said Pravin is married, didn't you?"

"Yes Sir. He's been married since ten years now and has two kids. We got it from one source that Pravin has a soft corner for her, which corresponds with what we've heard, since he's the one who keeps going to meet her."

"Interesting. Even Priya Karhadkar told us that Pravin dropped in on the night of 24th July. He didn't make any mention of that in his statement. That fellow is surely concealing something."

"He's got much to be embarassed about Sir. Pravin and Nilesh are both corrupt guys. They have a reputation for compromising on ethics. I've even heard that Pravin had a reputation for being bullied by clients, which is quite unusual for an auditor. But its quite the opposite in his office, where I hear he plays the bully."

"That's typical with such guys. The most servile chaps are also the most vicious bullies when they're in a position of power. Anyway, I must say those guys in Shilahar are pretty efficient. What else did they get?"

"That's about it Sir. There's one small detail which could be of some consequence. I believe Nilesh once had a fight with someone. More accurately, that other fellow, Wamanrao Kamble, had a physical altercation with Nilesh in his own office."

"Physical? What was that one about?"

"Apparently, Nilesh signed a document that Kamble's company owed money so some company called Consit Engineers. Kamble claimed that no such money was due. From what we've heard, that fellow went to Nilesh's office to confront him on the matter. Apparently he was drunk that day and Kamble bashed him in a fit of anger."

"Interesting. Our man seems to be world beaten. Anything else Manish?"

"That's all we have right now Sir. We've just received the mobile records of Nilesh, Priya and Pravin. Hopefully, we should get some more clues there."

"What about the car? Any update on it?"

"No Sir. We got the chassis number this morning. The details have been circulated to all the police stations in our state."

"I guess its still early days. Hopefully we should soon hear about the car. Nonetheless, we've made good progress so far. We've not only identified the body, but even have a couple of suspects. Great work Manish."

"Thank you Sir. how do we take this further from here? Should we call Pravin?"

"No Manish. Not yet. Let's get information on their call records first. Let's have as much on hand as possible before we confront them."

"Right Sir."

Skeletons Out of
the Cupboard

Hrishi's extension started ringing. "Hello?" said he, picking up the receiver.

"Sir Manish here. Are you free now?"

"*Haan aa ja,*" replied Hrishi. "*Haan* Deshpande?" asked he, as Manish entered his cabin a couple of minutes later.

"Sir I've taken a thorough look at the phone records of Nilesh, Pravin and Priya and there are some interesting findings which could be of some significance."

"Okay, tell me."

"I'll start with Nilesh Sir. Here's his call record. First and foremost, there isn't a single call to anyone by the name of Ravi Dixit."

"Okay! So either Nilesh or Priya, one of the two have lied... Anyway, carry on."

"Another thing I noticed is this Sir. Look at the frequency of calls to this number I have highlighted in green."

Hrishi whistled. "Whose number is it?"

"Some lady called Nehal Patel. We have tried contacting her but her mobile is now switched off."

"Where's she from?"

"She's from Kanheda Sir."

"Interesting. Is she the 'Ravi Dixit' that Nilesh was supposed to be meeting?"

"Looks like it Sir. Incidentally, the last known location of Nilesh's mobile was somewhere close to Kanheda. He moved out of the city just before the mobile was switched off."

"What time was it switched off?"

"At 7:43 P.M on 24th July."

"Hmm. Looks like this Patel woman might know a thing or two. Get her address Manish, we need to speak to her."

"I already have her address Sir."

"Great. What else do we have Manish?"

"If you see Sir, the other numbers which appear repeatedly are of Pravin and to a lesser extent, Priya. But there are two other numbers which appear quite frequently. There's this one- some fellow called Mohammed Rafique. Then there's another number here. If you look at the records, there have been a lot of calls to and from this number in the last month or so before 24th July. Its some fellow called Ashish Goyal."

"I see. *Sabhi ki kundli nikal Manish*. Anything else?"

"Yes Sir. There was also a call from this number on the evening of 24th July. They spoke for two minutes and forty three seconds."

"Whose number is it?"

"Wamanrao Kamble Sir."

"I see! Anything else Manish?"

"Yes Sir, there's this number. Nilesh received only one call from this number on 24th July. The conversation lasted less than a minute. It was the last call to or from Nilesh's number. That number is now switched off. Its some chap called Shijo Alexander."

"Who's he?"

"No idea Sir, I've asked for the call records. No such name has turned up in our investigation so far."

"Could be a wrong number then. What else Manish?"

"That's it from Nilesh's records, though I still need to take a more detailed look. As for Priya Karhadkar and Pravin Kumar's

21

call records, there's only one noticeable pattern. I've highlighted the number of times they've spoken to each other, look," said Manish, putting the paper on the table.

Hrishi whistled. *"Ilu ilu chal raha hai kya?* Interestingly, its Pravin who's been making the calls, not Priya."

"Yes Sir. If you see, Both were in Shilahar on 24th July Sir. Neither of them left the city anytime that day and neither of them have a second number."

"I see. So we can safely rule out their presence at the crime scene that night. *Ek kaam kar boss*, get the mobile phone records of that Patel lady. And those other fellows: Rafique, Kamble and Goyal, *unke aur is Nehal Patel ka pura kundli nikal.*"

"Sure Sir."

"Anything else Manish?"

"Just one small detail Sir. Pravin's mobile phone was in Kanheda on 26th July."

"26th July? What the hell was he doing there? Well I guess... anyway, fantastic work Manish, keep it up."

A Murky Affair

Manish was seated in Hrishi's cabin, waiting for his senior officer to return to his seat. Presently, Hrishi came back. Having washed his face, he looked noticeably fresher than he did a few minutes ago.

"Good evening Sir, looks like you had a hard day."

"Hard it was. The route from Pritampur was a horrible one. Anyway, what up? Looks like you've been waiting for me."

"Yes Sir. Its regarding the Kanheda murder case."

"Okay. What's up on that one?"

"Sir you'd remember that there were several calls between Nilesh and this lady called Nehal Patel. This Patel lady happens to be from Pune."

"Pune!"

"Yes Sir. she's a chartered accountant and she did her articleship in a firm called S.M. Prabhu & Associates, which happens to be the same firm in which Nilesh and Pravin did their articles."

"Ah! So the connection goes a long way back."

"Yes Sir. She started her articleship in 1998, which is a year after Nilesh and Pravin started. I got it from Pune that there was something going on between her and Nilesh."

"I see. So were they seeing each other?"

"Not exactly Sir. Nilesh was apparently interested in her, but the sentiment was one sided."

Okay. So there was more than just a professional rapport between then. Interesting... what else?"

"Sir Nehal qualified as CA in 2003 and she got married in 2005."

"Married? So she's married."

"And divorced Sir. the divorce happened in 2008."

"What's the name of her ex-husband?"

"Manohar Mariappa."

"South Indian name... looks like a love marriage gone wrong."

Manish nodded "That's the impression the colleagues at work have. From the little that we've managed to find, she's hardly in contact with her ex-husband. They don't have any children either."

"Hmm. I wonder... it looks like Nilesh was having an affair with her. If he was, then the question arises, did Priya know about it? If she didn't, it would explain the difference between her statment and our findings."

"Yes Sir. We'll need to speak to her about it."

"The other question is, what on earth was Pravin doing in Kanheda on the 26th? Has he done this in collusion with her?"

"We'll need to find out Sir. It doesn't look likely, since there are no calls from his mobile to hers. There are many calls from their office landline to her number, but they could have also been made by Nilesh."

"Hmm. Let's have a word with Pravin. Also get the addresses of all the other fellows that Nilesh spoke to. I'll go and meet all of them."

"Okay Sir. Incidentally, I've got Nehal's call records. I haven't had the time to go through them, but I'll discuss it with you as soon as I get the time."

"Fine, go ahead Manish. We're making good progress. This Nehal Patel holds the key. Nilesh had most probably gone to see her when he disappeared. She should know a thing or two. We'll look her up Manish. could you send Asha here?"

"Sure Sir."

The Plot Thickens

A SI Asha was at the wheel. Seated next to her was Manish, who looking for 7th road in Subhash Nagar where Nehal Patel lived.

"Look there," said Manish. "The next left."

"Ji Sir," said Asha. She turned left. They didn't need to look far to find Plot No.6. Asha parked the car. The two stepped out. The gate was shut but not locked. Manish opened it and entered the compound followed by Asha. He rang the doorbell.

There was no reply.

He rang the bell again.

Still no reply.

"*Chakkar kya hai*. Looks like she's not here, but her car is still parked inside the gate."

Just a moment, let me check," said Asha. She dialled Nehal Patel's number on her mobile phone. "Still switched off Sir," said she, shaking her head.

"Have you noticed those two ladies who are looking here?" asked Manish.

"Yes Sir," replied Asha, looking around without making it obvious.

"Check with them Asha. They'll be more comfortable talking to a lady officer,"

"Okay Sir." Asha walked over to the wall seperating the plot from the neighbour's house. "Hello madam. I'm ASI Asha Kadam from Madhavgadh crime branch. I need your help," said she in Hindi.

25

"Namaste madam," said the other lady. "how can I help you?" asked the lady in Hindi.

"What's your name?"

"Ruchi Sinha," came the reply.

"You see Ruchiji, we are looking for Nehal Patel. We understand she lives here. Would you know where we could find her?"

"She works in some company here. But I haven't seen her in a long time."

"How long?"

"Must be a month now. Kyon Shilpa?" asked Ruchi, raising her voice so that she could be heard by the lady from the other house, which was located two plots away from the other side, who was watching them.

"*Kya?*" asked Shilpa Sharma.

"Shilpaji, I'm ASI Asha from Madhavgadh Crime Branch. Can you please come here?" asked Asha.

"Okay," said Shilpa. She rather reluctantly joined her neighbour Ruchi.

"I understand you haven't seen Nehal Patel since the last few days. When did you last see her?"

"Must be a month, kyon Shilpa?" asked Ruchi Sinha. Shilpa nodded. "*Mahine ke upar hi hoga madam.*"

"You have any idea where she went?" The two ladies looked at each other. The blank expression said it all. "Can you remember when you last saw her?" asked Asha, not bothering to wait for the confirmation. Ruchi Sinha shook her head. "You Shilpaji?" asked Asha, turning to Shilpa.

"The last time I saw her was sometime in July. It was the day on which it rained heavily. I remember because I got delayed while coming back from office due to the rains."

"That day? I..."

"Please wait Ruchiji, we'll come to you in a moment," said Asha. "Did you see her that day?" asked she, turning to Shilpa.

26

"Yes Madam. I remember seeing that fellow leave. He was here once or twice before. He was leaving when I reached home. That should have been around seven. Nehal was at the gate to see him off."

"Was it this man?" asked Asha, retreiving the picture of Nilesh in her mobile phone.

"Yes Ma'am, it was this fellow. *Kaise aapne...*"

"Never mind. So you saw this fellow leave?"

"Yes Ma'am. He left in his car."

"Was it a Tata Safari?"

Shilpa nodded. "I was driving back from office in my scooty when I saw that fellow at the gate waving out to Nehal."

"Okay. What happened then?"

"Nothing ma'am, he left and I saw Nehal go back in."

"Was he alone or was there anyone with him?"

"No idea ma'am. It was too dark, since we still don't have street lighting here. I didn't even see the other car that night."

"What other car?" asked Asha, visibly confused.

"There was another car just behind that fellow's vehicle. That driver was driving with his headlights off. I didn't see him until he was really close. He splashed water all over my dress, bloody fellow."

"So that was the last time you saw her?"

"Her and him. I never saw either of them after that."

"What about you Ruchiji? You saw her that day?"

"Not really, but I remember that day because of the rains. Nehal went out that night."

"What time was it?"

"Should have been around 7:30 I think. I'm not sure of the time. I happened to be at the balcony on the upper floor when I saw her car move out of the gate."

"Was she alone or was there someone with her?"

"There was someone with her. I remember seeing this big, tall fellow with a beard step out of the car to close the gate. I remember that clearly because I was surprised to see a stranger getting off from the driver's side."

"A stranger? You haven't seen him before?"

"I didn't see his face ma'am, it was too dark for that, but it was a very tall and hefty fellow. There's no one like that in this area and I don't ever remember seeing anyone like that here. As it is, Nehal very rarely had visitors."

"I see. So that was the last you saw her?"

"No ma'am, she came back later that night."

"What time?"

"I don't remember madam. I was putting my book back in the shelf, which is close to the window. That's when I saw the car come back."

"Was that other man with her then?"

"I didn't see ma'am."

"And you never saw Nehal Patel after that?"

"No ma'am."

"Okay. What about the other neighbours? Would anyone else know?"

"There are only three houses here on this road which are occupied Madam. These houses are all new. This area has only recently been developed. All the other plots on this road are empty as of now, except those under constrution houses you can see here."

"Okay. What about Nehal Patel? Did she own this house?"

"I don't know Madam.."

"Did she live alone or was there anyone else living here?"

"No she was alone."

"And visitors?"

"Like I said, she rarely had any visitors except that fellow whose photo you showed."

"And that other fellow with whom she went out that night."

"Yes ma'am, that other fellow. Otherwise I don't remember seeing anyone else."

Shilpa nodded in agreement.

"How is she as a person?"

"She never speaks to anyone. All I know is that she works at the cement factory."

"There's one more thing," said Ruchi. "I'd forgotten about it, but I suddenly remembered."

"What's it?" asked Manish.

"Sir there was this fellow who came some days ago inquiring about Nehal."

"When was it?"

"I'm not Sure, but it must be two- three weeks now. He wanted to meet Nehal. I told him that she wasn't at home and I hadn't seen Nehal over the past few days."

"Did he give you his name?"

"No Sir. I asked him who he was. He only told me that he was an old friend who had planned to give her a surprise."

"What did he look like?"

Ruchi pondered for a moment. "I think he was dark, fat and he wore glasses. That's all I can remember."

"I see. Well, thank you very much. I may have to contact you again. Please give me your mobile numbers," said Asha.

Manish, who had gone back to the car and taken the driver's seat saw Asha approaching the vehicle in the rear view mirror. Presently the door opened and Asha took her seat next to him.

"So what's up?"

"*Gadbad hai Sir.* the neighbours are saying that they haven't seen Nehal Patel in over a month now."

"I see. Since when?"

"No one seems to remember the exact date, but it happened to be the day it rained heavily."

"That should be 24th July," said Manish. "It rained very heavily that night. So Nehal has been missing since the same night."

"Yes Sir. Interestingly, one of the ladies saw Nehal go out with another chap that same night."

"Who?"

"No idea Sir. She couldn't see his face, but she said that it was a very tall and hefty chap with a beard. Apparently there's no one like that in this area, so it was an outsider."

"I see. Which way did they go?"

"That way Sir. She told me that she saw the car come back some time later that night."

"Was she alone or was that other fellow with her then?"

"She didn't pay much attention Sir. she just got a glimpse of the car."

"Any idea what time it was?"

"They seem to have left around half past 7. Not sure about the time they returned."

"Hmm. So Nehal disappeared the same night on which Nilesh was murdered. The question now is, is there a connection between the two?"

"Should be Sir. Its too much of a coincidence that both of them disappeared the same night."

"That's true Asha, the circumstances suggest that there is a strong connection between the two. But... tell me, was Nilesh here that day?"

"Yes Sir, he was. The other lady I spoke to saw him coming out of the gate when she was returning from work."

"What time was that?"

"Around seven in the evening Sir."

"Seven in the evening. Hmm, so let's try and reconstruct what happened that night. Nilesh leaves around 7. Nehal goes out with someone else a short while later. Then she and this other fellow are seen coming back together some time later- hour not sure."

"Sir, maybe they went and murdered Nilesh."

"Maybe, but it looks unlikely Asha. They drove that way and Nilesh should have gone in the exact opposite direction to get to the toll naka where the operator remembered seeing him. Besides, they left about half an hour after him. Could they have caught up with him... or is there a short cut from the opposite direction? Let's check it out Asha."

"Okay Sir."

Manish drove in the direction that Ruchi Sinha had indicated. It was a very narrow road that presently gave way to a rough pathway. They continued driving down that road for a long time before the road abruptly came to a dead end.

"Hello! Just the woods ahead." said Manish. Asha shook her head, looking clearly nonplussed. "Did you see a turning anywhere?"

"No Sir, I didn't."

"Neither did I. They couldn't have gone anywhere. What the hell were they doing here?"

"Don't know Sir. Don't understand."

"That means... either they have nothing to do with the Nilesh murder or there is a third guy who was with them."

"Maybe. Wait, you're right Sir. That other lady said that there was a vehicle just behind Nilesh' car. He was apparently driving with the headlights off, so she didn't see the car. He seems to have splashed water on her dress."

"Okay! So there were indeed two guys. That means we are looking at Nehal Patel plus two guys who were involved with her in this racket, out of which one was a very tall and hefty fellow with a beard. We'll need to find out more about this lady Asha. She surely has the answers to our questions."

"What do we do now Sir?"

"Let's go to her office first."

Visit to Nehal's Office

M anish was ushered into the cabin of Shardul Sonawane, HR Manager at Diamond Cement Ltd. "Good afternoon officer. How can I help you?" asked he.

"Hello Mr. Sonawane. I'm Inspector Manish Deshpande from Madhavgadh Crime Branch. I'm here to inquire about Ms. Nehal Patel. I understand she's an employee of your company."

"That's true Sir. She's one of our employees. What would you like to know?"

"Where is she presently?"

"Don't know Sir. its been over a month since she reported to work. We filed a missing persons complaint with the police, but we have got no reply from them."

"Which police station was it?"

"Sir Subhash Nagar police station."

"I see. When did Nehal Patel last report to work?"

"22nd July Sir. she was on leave for 23rd and 24th. She was to resume on the 25th, but never turned up."

"Did you receive any communication from her?"

"No Sir. I checked up with everyone in the company. None of them had heard from her. We tried every possible means of contacting her. We got in touch with all her known friends. We even managed to trace down her ex-husband, but we he had no idea where she was and he didn't sound particularly interested either."

"I see. What kind of person was Nehal?"

"She usually stuck to her work Sir. Hardly used to talk to anyone. She was hardworking and pretty good at her work, but not very sociable. I can say with certainty that there's no one here who disliked her, but I doubt if anyone here would have an opinion about her."

"Any friends here?"

"No Sir. Nehal was here for about a year. She never befriended anyone during that time."

"I see. Alright Mr. Mohite, I want copies of all the documents pertaining to Nehal Patel that you have, including her CV."

"Sure Sir. I'll arrange for it."

———◈———

Manish and Asha entered the premises of Subhash Nagar police station. "Ji?" asked a policeman.

"I'm Inspector Manish Deshpande from Madhavgadh Crime Branch. I want to see your SHO."

"One minute Sir. Please be seated," replied the other man.

They were presently ushered into the cabin of the Station House Officer Shankar Prakash. "Good afternoon," said he, getting up and shaking hands with Manish. "What brings the crime branch team here all the way from Madhavgadh?"

"Good afternoon Prakash saahab. We're here to inquire about a lady called Nehal Patel. I understand there's a missing complaint about her in this police station."

"Nehal Patel...was it that Gujju lady working in that cement company?"

"That's the one Prakash saahab."

"I don't remember offhand. Let me get the file. Too many things happening- I'll remember when I see it."

"Please."

The file was brought in by a constable. SHO Shankar Prakash quickly browsed through the contents. "Oh yes, this case. I remember this one. The complaint was filed by the HR fellow in her company."

"I just met him a short while ago Prakash Saahab. I'm sure you would have looked into this matter. Could you tell me what you found."

"To be honest Deshpande saahab, we got nowhere. We checked out all the toll nakas. We also circulated the photographs to all the railway stations. If this lady ran away, she should have crossed at least one of those points, but no one remembered seeing her. There were no transactions on her credit card or her bank account. She's just vanished like that, without a trace."

"That's strange. Is there any money in her bank account?"

"More than two lakh rupees Deshpande saahab, apart from FDs and mutual fund investments worth 12-13 lakhs. Her accounts are under surveillance, but there hasn't been a single transaction for over a month. The last transaction was an ATM withdrawal of three thousand rupees on 9th July."

"Okay..." said Manish, perplexed. "That's strange. I believe she went out with some tall fellow on the night when he disappeared."

"And came back too, that too in her car. We know that Deshpande saahab, but we haven't been able to identify that man. I checked out her colleagues in office, but none of them fit the description. There's another fellow who used to come to see her in a Tata Safari, but he didn't fit the description. In any case, he left well before the neighbour saw that other fellow, so there's no point even trying to trace him."

"That's Nilesh Karhadkar," said Manish. "He was murdered on 24th July Prakash saahab. His body was thrown into the river and it was found the next morning."

"The same day on which this lady disappeared!"

"That's right. We have reason to believe that the two events are connected. We actually came here investigating the murder of that man Nilesh. From what we know, it appears that this lady Nehal Patel might have a hand in the murder."

"Okay...What's this all about Deshpande Saahab? This is something we're completely unaware of."

Manish quickly summarised the chain of events leading to the present.

"My God!" exclaimed Prakash. "I never knew there's such a complicated tale associated with this lady.

"Its only getting more and more complicated Prakash Saahab. Do you have any idea what Nehal Patel and that other man did that night?

Prakash shook his head. "No idea Sir. We too checked out that route and I promise you, we scouted every inch of that road, but we were unable to find out what they were upto that night. there's absolutely nothing on that road right now. Of course, things will change a lot when they finally extend it to join NH 16. The work should have started last winter, but there's no movement on that yet."

"Okay, I wasn't aware of that, though its of no consequence to our case. The thing is, its getting even more complicated now. It looks like Nehal Patel conspired with two guys to get rid of Nilesh for whatever reason. Perhaps it was she with someone else and the third guy was paid for his service."

"Quite possible Deshpande saahab, it fits well with what we know so far. She might have run away to avoid arrest."

"Most likely, yes. The question now is, how on earth do we trace her down? Her mobile is switched off and no one seems to have the least idea where she could be, unless..."

"Unless?"

"Unless we keep a tab on the people with whom she regularly interacted. We'll need your help for that Prakashji."

"No problem Deshpande saahab. Just let me know *kis kiske kundli nikalne hai*."

"Let me discuss this with my senior officer Prakash saahab. I'll get back to you on this."

"You're most welcome."

Another Lead

Hrishi's mobile phone started ringing. "Hello?" said he, taking the call.

"Hello, am I speaking to ACP Bharadwaj?"

"Yes, speaking..."

"Hello ji, I'm SHO Sonawane from Kalika police station in Pritampur."

"Hello Sonawaneji," said Hrishi. Why on earth was this guy calling him?

"Bharadwajji, we have got information regarding that Tata Safari you were looking for."

"Oh great. Is it in your city?" asked Hrishi, still trying to figure out which car Sonawane was talking about.

"Yes boss. The number is changed, but one of our informers recognised the chasis number the moment it came to his garage."

"Ok! Where's the garage?" asked Hrishi, finally understanding the context.

"Its Dattatreya Auto Garage in Vakholi. You can take down the name and number," said Sonawane. Hrishi jotted down the details and thanked Sonawane. He instantly dialed Manish's number.

"Hello Sir," came the familiar voice from the other end.

"Hi Manish. Still in Kanheda?"

"Yes Sir, we're about to finish, we've..."

"Its okay, tell me about it later boss. I'm upto my neck in the Dhanraj murder case. I've just got a lead on the Kanheda murder case, can you take it up?"

"Sure Sir."

"I just got a call from SHO Sonawane in Pritampur. Apparently Nilesh's car was spotted by an informer of theirs called Raju. I just got his number. Just take it down, will you?"

"Sure Sir, tell me."

Hrishi read out the number from the piece of paper on which he had hurriedly jotted it down. Manish read it out, gesturing to Asha to note it down.

It was around one in the afternoon the following day, when Manish and Govind Mane entered Dattatreya Auto Garage in Pritampur.

"Ji Sir?" asked a garage worker, seeing the two strangers enter.

"I want to see Raju," said Manish in Hindi.

"Raju? He's there Sir, by that car. Are Raju, there's a visitor for you," shouted out the mechanic to a thin, underweight mechanic across the room.

"Ji Sir?" asked Raju, walking up to Manish.

"I'm Inspector Manish Deshpande from Madhavgadh Crime Branch. We were informed by SHO Sonawane that you saw the Safari we're looking for."

"Oh that one. Yes sir, that car came to our garage yesterday. Look its there," said Raju.

"Mane, take a look," said Manish. Govind Mane went with Raju.

"*Wohi gaadi hai Sir,*" said Mane, walking back to Manish, followed by Raju.

"Who brought this car here Raju?"

"Ramesh saahab can tell you," said Raju, pointing to an air conditioned cabin in which a bespetacled man was seated.

"Okay. Thank you very much Raju," said Manish. he nodded to Govind Mane. The two entered the cabin.

"Ji?" asked the bespectacled man.

"*Namaste Rameshji*, I'm Inspector Manish Deshpande from Madhavgadh Crime Branch. I want to know who brought that Tata Safari car there and his contact details."

"Sure officer, please be seated."

◆◆◆◆◆◆

About half an hour later, Manish and Govind entered the office of Good Homes real estate agency. "Yes Sir?" asked the lady at the reception.

"I want to see Akhilesh Bhatnagar."

"He's with a client Sir."

"Ask him to come ma'am. I'm from crime branch."

"Okay Sir, please wait."

"Yes officer, I'm Akhilesh Bhatnagar" said a tall, paunchy man who entered the room. Although he was just in his mid thirties, he looked nearer forty.

"I'm Inspector Manish Deshpande from Madhavgadh Crime Branch."

"Good afternoon Sir. What brings officers from the other end of the state to my office?"

"Your Tata Safari Mr. Bhatnagar."

"*Kya hua usko*? Has it been..."

"Mr. Bhatnagar, get me your car papers."

"Papers? They're lying at home Sir."

"Have them brought over immediately."

"But why Sir."

"Mr. Bhatnagar, your car is a stolen car and the previous owner was murdered. If the car is yours, then I have reason to suspect that you had a hand in the murder."

"Sir I..." started Bhatnagar, visibly scared.

"Tell me the truth Bhatnagar. It'll be much easier for both of us."

"Sir I bought it from a garage. *Mere paas koi paper vaper nahi hai.*"

"Which Garage?"

"Bali Garage Sir. Its near Netaji Chowk."

"Come with us there," said Manish.

"Sir I have a client here..."

"Tell him that you have to leave in an emergency."

"Can it wait just a few minutes Sir?"

"Will you do it yourself or do you want us to tell your client that we're taking you with us."

"Just one minute Sir," said Bhatnagar with a browbeaten face.

Manish, Govind and Akhilesh Bhatnagar entered the premises of Bali Garage.

"Namaste saahab," said a mechanic, seeing Bhatnagar. Evidently he was a well known face there.

"I want to see Bali," said Manish.

"Ji Sir?"

"I'm Inspector Manish Deshpande from Crime Branch. Call Bali here now," said Manish.

Presently an aging man in his fifties with a beer belly and a beard came rushing to Manish. The servile look on his face gave the impression of a coward and bully. "Ji saahab?"

"Bali, I'm here regarding the Tata Safari you sold to Bhatnagar Saahab."

"Which one."

"*Are, wohi jo maine pichle mahine liya tha,*" said Akhilesh Bhatnagar.

"*Sir woh...*"

"Look Bali, I'm here regarding a murder investigation. That car belongs to the fellow who got murdered. It was missing all these days. Mr. Bhatnagar tells me that you sold it to him without any papers. So tell me why did you murder Nilesh?"

"Sir I don't know any Nilesh. I just bought this car from Bandya."

"Who's he?"

"Sir Bandya gets these goods from different places and sells it to others."

"And you think I'm a fool to believe all this."

"Really Sir. I'm just a businessman. I got an offer to buy a Tata Safari 2009 model for just two lakhs. How could I let it go?"

"Two lakhs!" exclaimed Bhatnagar. He was about to say something, but Manish cut him short.

"I want Bandya *now*. You'll take me to his place."

"Sir he doesn't have a fixed place. I can call him here if you want."

"Call him right now. And don't even by mistake tell him that we're here. *Chalaki ki toh sochna bhi mat. Sidha encounter ho jayega.*"

"No Sir, please. I'll call him right away," said Bali, visibly frightened.

Manish and Govind were seated in Bali's cabin when Bandya entered about an hour later. "Namaste Sir," said he, greeting both officers who were not in uniform. "What did you want?"

"You," said Manish, nodding to Govind, who got up and stood by the door, ensuring that Bandya could not run away just in case the thought entered his mind.

"Me?" asked Bandya, beginning to sense trouble.

"Yes you. Where did you get the Tata Safari that you sold him?"

"What Safari?"

Raju had barely posed the question when Mane grabbed him by the collar and pulled out his revolver. "Just answer the questions saahab asks you. *Zyaada shanpatti dikhayega to sidhe uda denge tereko.*"

"Sir..."

"Where did you get the car? Talk fast Bandya, officer Govind here likes bashing people. *Isne bade bade khiladiyon ka muh khulwaya hai.* I don't want any unnecessary *maar peet* here."

"Sir I don't know the fellow..."

"Which fellow? Give the the full details boss. Don't test my patience."

"Sir, some weeks ago a big guy with a beard called me up. He was a giant Sir, he must have been six and a half feet."

"When was this?"

"I'm not sure of the date Sir, but it must have been around 5th August, because it was before I went to my village."

"How did that guy get to know about you?"

"I don't know Sir. he just called me up and told me that he had a Tata Safari to sell, which was in excellent condition. He asked to meet me, so I went personally to Shivaji Nagar market to meet this chap. He took me to a corner where the car was parked."

"Who was he?"

"I don't know him Sir. I've never seen him before or since. He told me that his name was Deepak."

"Which was obviously a false name. Where did he come from? Where did he get the car?"

"I don't know Sir. He didn't tell me, I didn't ask."

"Do you have his number?"

"No Sir. he called me just once. I had no reason to save his number."

"Do you remember his face? Can you help an artist make a sketch?"

"I... sorry Sir, but I can't. This was almost a month ago. I meet so many people..." replied Bandya, almost shrinking at the nasty glare Manish gave him.

Manish shook his head in annoyance. Yet another trail had gone dead.

Nehal's Phone Records

Manish took his seat opposite Hrishi. "Tell me boss," said the ACP.

"Sir I came to update you on the Kanheda murder case."

"Oh yes boss. I'd even forgotten that, thanks to this RTI activist case. Anyway, tell me. What did you get?"

"For starters Sir, this lady Nehal Patel has been missing since 24th July."

"24th July? That's the same day!"

"Yes Sir. I've got the mobile records too. Nilesh's mobile went off at 7:43 P.M that night and Nehal's mobile was switched off at 7:28 P.M."

"Around the same time. So, both of them disappeared the very same night and their mobile phones too were switched off almost at the same time."

"Yes Sir. The two are surely connected. We have issued a red alert for Nehal. Unfortunately, we haven't got a clue as to where she went. The local police checked all the toll points, railway stations and the nearest airport. She should have surely crossed at least one of those points, but there was no ticket issued either by railways or by any of the airlines in the name of Nehal Patel and none of the guys at any of the toll gates remembered seeing her."

"She could have easily slipped below the radar. Think of it boss, there must be hundreds, possibly thousands passing through the toll naka everyday. After a month, what are the chances that anyone would remember one random person out of those thousands?"

"True Sir. From what we know, there were two others with Nehal Patel who were involved in this. We spoke to her neighbours Sir, there are only two other houses in that street which are occupied. Both of them remembered seeing her that night."

"Okay, what else did you get from them?"

"One of them remembered seeing Nilesh leaving around seven that night when she was returning from work. She added that there was another guy behind, who was driving with his headlights off. She didn't notice that car in the darkness and apparently he splashed water on her. Now if he splashed on her, he was obviously moving. He was most probably following Nilesh. He could be the one who murdered him."

"Sounds plausible."

"There was another man Sir, some tall and hefty *daadhiwala* with whom another neighbour saw Nehal go out around the same time. She even remembered seeing the car come back some time later the same night."

"Hmm. So Nehal goes out somewhere, then comes back, but she switches off her mobile phone before that and then disappears altogether after returning home."

"Yes Sir. Incidentally, she went out in her car that night. The car was parked inside the gates of her house when we went. It was lying there for over a month."

"What on earth was going on then? She goes out in her car then comes back home, then she leaves her car behind and just vanishes... it just doesn't make sense."

"Its even more bizzare Sir. Asha and I checked out the route on which they went out that night. that road leads nowhere and we didn't see any road joining or branching out."

"This makes no sense at all. Was the neighbour making it all up?"

"That's what even I suspected Sir, but in the light of what we've learnt, I don't think so. But there's one more detail which I ought to mention. I don't know if its of any relevance, but one of the neighbours told us that a stranger came inquiring about Nehal a few days after she disappeared."

"A stranger? Who?"

"We haven't able to find out Sir. She couldn't remember his face well enough."

"Okay."

"But coming back to what I was saying Sir, as you're aware, I'd been to Pritampur yesterday."

"Oh yes, what did you get there?"

"We managed to trace it from the garage down to the fence in Pritampur who sold it, a guy called Bandya who's a history sheeter himself. He didn't know the chap who sold it to him. Apparently he introduced himself as Deepak, which surely wasn't his real name."

"That's fairly obvious."

"He didn't have that Deepak's contact details, but he remembered one useful little detail which tallies with what we've got so far."

"What's that?"

"That Deepak fellow is a tall guy- Bandya said that he must be around six and a half feet. He's hefty and has a beard."

"The same fellow! That leaves no doubt that Nilesh's murder and Nehal's disappearance are connected."

"Yes Sir, the two are definitely connected. So we have two guys on the radar: this Patel lady herself and this big bearded chap."

"What about the person who murdered Nilesh? You're missing him."

"We have no idea who he was Sir. We don't know what car he was driving and we have no description of that chap either. I'm not even sure where to begin looking for that fellow."

"Ya, you're right."

"There's just one more important fact Sir. Apparently Nehal's phone has now been switched on under a different number. We should be getting the details in a day or two."

"Okay great. You said you got her call records too, didn't you?"

"Yes Sir. For starters, the last location was the same area as her residence, which means she was most likely at home when the mobile was switched off."

"Okay."

"As far as the records go, there were frequent calls to and from three numbers apart from Nilesh. We checked out all of them. One of them was the nearby kiranawallah. I've already spoken to that fellow. Apparently, that fellow offers home delivery."

"Which explains the number of calls to that number."

"Yes Sir. The other was her boss. Nehal worked as Regional Finance Manager in Diamond Cements. They have their regional headquarters in Kanheda."

"Kanheda?"

"Yes Sir. Since there are vast limestone deposits thereabouts, they have their plant and regional headquarters in that city."

"I see. Alright. Where's her boss based?"

"He's based in the company's Head Office in Mumbai. That's the GM Finance, Mr. Advait Paranjpe, to whom she was reporting."

"Okay, that's understandable. What about the third number?"

"That's Dr. Nitin Balakrishnan, her dentist."

"Her dentist?"

"Yes Sir. He's based in Kanheda. I called him up. He told me that Nehal was undergoing root canaling. She had to reschedule her appointments repeatedly due to professional commitments."

"Okay, so that goes some way into explaining it. Anything else?"

"Yes Sir, there were a couple of calls from this number here. It happens to be that of Manohar Mariappa."

"Her ex-husband?"

"Yes Sir. he's based in Mumbai. Interestingly, the first call was on 21st July and the second one was on 23rd July."

"Around the time of her disappearance."

"Yes Sir. it could be a coincidence, but it could also mean that he is in some way involved in this matter. I've got in touch with the guys in Mumbai. Let's see what we get from there."

"Hmm. There's one thing which makes no sense to me boss. What motive could Nehal have to get rid of Nilesh? From what we know, its obvious that its a very well planned murder. But why would she do that? Was there money involved?"

"No Sir. We checked out both their bank records, there was no suspicious transaction. She didn't even take money out of her accounts, her FDs and mutual funds add up to more than ten lakhs and there's more than one lakh in her account. She hasn't touched her money."

"Which means it wasn't money, but something else. Anyway, I'll take a day out for this case. Let's go to Shilahar and look up Pravin and the others tomorrow."

Meeting with Ashish Goyal

Hrishi was seated in the meeting room of Dixons Chemicals Pvt. Ltd. The office was a well lit, spacious and rather new one. The meeting room was just a small glass cubicle with a table at the centre which could at best accomodate two people.

The office boy had only just left a glass of tea for the guest when the door opened and an overweight and somewhat boyish looking fellow entered. "Hi, I'm Ashish Goyal," said he. There was a big smile on his face. Although he was in his over 40 now, Ashish looked no more than 35.

"Hello. I'm ACP Hrishikesh Bharadwaj from Madhavgadh Crime Branch."

"Hello Sir. what brings an officer all the way from Madhavgadh?" asked Ashish, visibly surprised.

"Its a murder case in Kanheda. I believe the victim was known to you."

"Ah, you're talking about the murder of Nilesh Karhadkar. Of course I should have figured it out."

"So my reputation preceeds me I see."

"Yes Sir. I got to know about it from Pravin. I was quite shocked to hear about it."

"Nilesh was your auditor, isn't it?"

Ashish nodded. "That's right Sir. They've been our auditors since four years now."

49

"I see. How was your relationship with Nilesh?"

"Good Sir. We are very happy with their service."

"You had plenty of interaction with him in June-July, didn't you?"

"Yes Sir. We wanted to finalise our financials as soon as possible."

"Okay. What about your partner Mr. Gupta? Was he also coordinating with Nilesh?"

"Not really. Rajiv has other business interests. In fact he spends most of his time in Dubai, where he has a lubricants business. I'm the one running the show here."

"I see. Is he in the country now?"

"No Sir. He had come down for a few days last month. He's back in the UAE now."

"I want his number."

"Sure," said Ashish. He pulled out his mobile phone from his pocket and fished out the number. "There," said he, handing his instrument to Hrishi.

"Thank you very much," said Hrishi. He quickly saved the number in his phone. "How about your personal equation with Nilesh?"

"Personal equation!" exclaimed Ashish, "I fear there was none officer. I knew him as our auditor and that was about it. You see Sir, one of the fundamental rules of business is that you don't mix pleasure with work. I can vouch for the fact that he was a very cooperative auditor. I never had any complaints about him, except for the fact that you had to get behind him for the audit finalisation, which is quite normal. How Nilesh was in his personal life, I have very little idea."

"What about his family?"

"I understand he has...had a two or three year old son. That's all I know Sir. Never met his family."

"And Pravin?"

"Don't know him too well. Nilesh was the one we have always dealt with. I've been forced to interact with him in the last few weeks. Thankfully most of the work was done. We managed to finalise the financials quickly."

"So you don't know him too well."

"To be honest, I hardly know him officer."

"So how did you get to know their firm?"

"I didn't know them Sir, it was Rajiv who called them up. I think he heard of Nilesh through a cousin of his who was from Pune."

"I see. I've heard that they didn't have a good reputation out there."

"I know what you're talking about officer. I've heard something similar, but my experience has been a bit different. Frankly, we're well established and our business is pretty straightforward, so I never had the occasion to try and use their services for anything out of the ordinary. I'm sure you'll understand what I mean."

Hrishi nodded. "I understand. Tell me Mr. Goyal, you spoke to Nilesh on the day he was murdered and you were one of the last few people who spoke to him. Did you sense anything out of the ordinary? Anything he may have said or the manner in which he spoke?"

"Not really. He only told me that he was out of town on some personal work. What it was, I had no idea. He didn't tell me or do anything that even remotely hinted that there was something amiss. In any case, I was quite likely the last person he would have remembered in an emergency. I wasn't exactly a friend of his."

"Alright. Tell me Mr. Ashish, what prompted you to call up Nilesh on a daily basis? Was the audit that important?"

"It was," replied Ashish. "We were planning to apply for a bank loan because we want to set up a new unit in Amravati. As you would be aware, audited financial statements are indispensable for that and Nilesh was taking his time over it. Unfortunately he disappeared and its only now that I've managed to get it finalised with Pravin. The whole episode has set us back by several months, because I'll have to wait for Rajiv to come to India. Unfortunately he's tied up with some other matter in Dubai right now, with the result that our project has got delayed at least till the winter."

"Alright."

"Anything else you would like to know Sir?"

"You have an employee here called Mohammed Rafique, isn't it?"

"Yes Sir, he's our finance manager."

"I'd like to have a word with him."

"Sure Sir. I'll arrange your meeting. Just a small request. Can I make a move? Not that I don't want to talk to you, but I've got a conf. call with an important client now."

"No problem."

Presently an office boy entered the cabin. "Please come this way Sir," said he.

"Okay," said Hrishi, taken aback somewhat. He was ushered into the cabin of Mohammed Rafique.

"Hello Sir, I'm sorry I couldn't come over to meet you. Unfortunately my foot is in a plaster," said Rafique. He was well built and probably a tall guy. He was clean shaven and had a dashing personality that would have made a model envious. Hrishi estimated him to be around the same age as him.

"No problem Rafique saahab," replied Hrishi. "I'm ACP Bharadwaj from Madhavgadh Crime Branch. I'm investigating the murder of Nilesh Karhadkar and we found that there were a lot of calls to him from your number."

"Yes Sir, that's right. We used to interact regularly."

"If I'm not mistaken, audit is an annual exercise, isn't it? So why the regular interaction?"

"Its true Sir, that an audit is an annual event. But Nilesh provided plenty of services other than audit. We keep requiring some certification or the other, for which I used to coordinate with him.

Even when audit wasn't on, I used to interact with him almost on a weekly basis."

"So you must be good friends?"

"Well Sir, an auditor is the most unwanted guy around. I mean, who'd want to have a guy around who's going to look at your work with a microscope and pick out your mistakes? He may have been a professional brother, but that was about it."

"Well, valid point."

"No offense meant Sir, but auditors and policemen can neither be friends, nor enemies."

Hrishi smiled. "Fair enough. So your relationship with Nilesh was purely a professional one."

"Yes Sir. We keep needing the services of our CAs for certifications and I promise you, in a line like this, we need it a lot more frequently than you would imagine. Besides, we had to keep pushing him, otherwise he would have taken his own sweet time."

"I see. What else do you know about him?"

"Not much Sir. I know he has a family and to my knowledge he also has a fondness for drinking. I've myself shared a drink with him once or twice."

"You must have been shocked to hear about the murder."

"I was Sir. Its always shocking to know that someone was murdered. Its one thing reading news articles, quite another when the murdered person happens to be someone you know."

"What kind of person was Nilesh?"

"Hard to say Sir. he was friendly with us, very coopearative. How he was in his personal life, I have no clue."

"Alright."

⋯⋘⋙⋯

In the meanwhile, Manish was in the office of Betacon Metals Pvt. Ltd to meet the Chairman of the company Mr. Wamanrao

Kamble. He was presently ushered into Kamble's cabin, where he found himself face to face with a dark, lean and bespetacled man. Kamble was good looking in a rugged kind of way.

"Good afternoon officer. Please be seated," said Kamble. "So how can I help you?"

"Well Mr. Kamble, I'm Inspector Manish Deshpande from Madhavgadh Crime Branch. I'm here regarding a murder investigation."

"Murder?" asked Kamble, taken aback.

"Yes Mr. Kamble. It's of a man called Nilesh Karhadkar. I understand you knew him."

"Oh that fellow? I knew he was going to get into trouble someday, but I never thought it would go so far," said Kamble. There was no mistaking the look of disgust on his face.

"So you knew him well."

"Not really officer, but I had the misfortune of having to interact with him, which left a poor taste in the mouth."

"What happened?"

"I had my office shifted here last year. You see, my business is expanding and our old premises at Nehru Nagar were inadequate. The entire design and building work was done by a contractor called Consit Constructions. Our contract provided for the last installment to be paid after completion and approval of the work done."

"Okay..."

"I was unhappy with the quality of the material used, especially in the canteen and the conference rooms. That bloody fellow Hitesh Jagasia who owns the company tried to cut corners using third rate material and shortchanged me. I naturally refused to pay the final installment."

"Okay," said Manish, still unable to understand how this could be connected to Nilesh.

"So that fellow tried to recover his dues by claiming that his company had given an advance of fifteen lakhs to mine. That Nilesh fellow, who's the auditor of Consit, issued a certificate that there was indeed such a transaction in the accounts of that company. Jagasia threatened to drag me to court using that certificate as evidence."

"And there was no such transaction?"

"None at all. It was bare faced cheating. I found out who the CA was and went to his office to discuss it with him. But that bloody bugger was drunk. He started abusing me. You see officer, I'm not a violent man, but I have quite a temper and I used to be a regular at the gym when I was younger. I just lost control. One slap and that fellow was down in a heap," said Kamble, barely able to conceal his anger.

"I see," said Manish, trying hard to prevent a smile from flickering on his lips. "When was this?"

"Second week of July. I tried talking sense into him, but it failed."

"So what happened?"

"I decided that if this guy wasn't playing ball, I'd drag him before the committee. I filed a case with the Institute of Chartered Accountants of India."

"You spoke to him on 24th July, didn't you?"

"That's right. I called up to inform him that I was hauling him up before the Institute's committee. He started pleading, but it was of no use."

"I see. What was exchanged between you?" asked Hrishi.

"I told him that I wasn't interested in hearing his views. Whatever he wanted to say, he could say it before the disciplinary committee hearing. That was about it. He was pleading repeatedly, till I lost my patience and disconnected."

"Okay, so that was it. Did you have any other interaction with him?"

"No officer. That was that. I guess its all of no consequence, now that Nilesh is dead. You said he's murdered?"

"That's right."

"Strange. I mean, I know that this Nilesh fellow was going to be in trouble some day. *Woh itna gaya guzra tha*, he would have put his hand into the commode if there was money to be had there. But I never imagined that he would be murdered."

"It has happened Mr. Kamble. Otherwise I wouldn't be here."

"I understand officer. Unfortunately, I can't be of much help to you. What I've told you is pretty much all that I know."

Manish nodded. It it was true, then there was little else to be gained. He would have to get some more information on Kamble.

"If there's anything else I can do for you, please let me know."

"I understand and appreciate Sir. I'll call you up if required. Thanks for your time," said Manish.

Pravin's Interrogation

Hrishi and Manish were seated in the meeting room of Karhadkar & Patel.

"*Sir kuch zyaada time nai laga raha hai?*" asked Manish.

"Never mind. *Bakre ko toh katna hi hai,* even if it takes a bit of time."

He had barely said it when the door opened and Pravin Kumar entered. "Good afternoon Sir," said he, "sorry I had to keep you waiting. I was on the phone with a client."

"No problem Pravin Saahab. Please be seated," said Hrishi. He gestured to Manish who took the cue. In a moment the door was locked.

"Why are you locking Sir?" asked Pravin, visibly perturbed.

"I don't want any interruptions Mr. Pravin. Please put your mobile in silent and keep it on the table. This is very serious business," said Hrishi, typically poker faced. There was a firm, almost hostile glint in his eye.

"Yes Sir," replied Pravin. He complied without question.

Hrishi got up from his seat and sat on the chair just next to Pravin's, sitting close to him. Manish took position right behind Pravin's chair, and remained standing.

"What's up Sir?" asked Pravin. Hrishi was pleased to see that he was beginning to feel intimidated, which was just the effect he wanted.

"I want you to tell me all that you know Pravin and fast!"

"But Sir, I told you everything that I knew."

"Look Pravin, I know you didn't tell me all. I want to hear the rest of the story."

"But..."

"Let's talk about Nehal Patel."

"Nehal Patel? I don't know her."

"How strange! You don't remember a former colleague with whom you did your articleship, whom you called some time ago- 2nd May to be precise- and who you went visiting on 26th July."

"Sir I don't know what you're talking about," said Pravin. His body language showed that he was clearly lying.

"Pravin, I've been nice with you so far, but we have other ways of getting information. Do you want us to humiliate you in front of your staff?"

"Sir I..." started Pravin, unable to go further.

"Look Pravin, I have your entire *janm kundli*, so don't waste my time. You've already wasted enough. Out now!" said Hrishi, speaking the last two words in a raised voice. He had moved even closer to Pravin. He was just a step away from treading on Pravin's toes.

"I'm sorry Sir," said Pravin, visibly intimidated. "But what could I do? I had no choice really."

"What happened?" asked Hrishi.

"Sir Nilesh was having an affair with Nehal."

"I know that. Since when?"

"I don't know Sir. But he had started seeing her regularly since March or April."

"March or April? Were they in regular touch before?"

"No Sir. We did our articleship together in the same CA firm. Nilesh had an eye on her even then, but she wasn't interested. We completely lost touch with her after we completed our articles. Suddenly, he found her online on Facebook sometime last year, about November or December. I still remember the day Nilesh told me that he'd managed to find Nehal on Facebook."

"And they were in regular contact thereafter?"

"Yes Sir, although I wasn't aware of it then. I mean, I knew that they were interacting regularly, but I never realised at first how far it had gone."

"When did you realise it?"

"Sometime in March. Nilesh started going out of town quite frequently. We don't have too many outstation audits, so I knew that something was not quite right, but I never realised how far it had gone until Priya told me about it."

"So she told you about it huh? *Chakkar kya hai boss*?"

"Sir she once used to be my girlfriend."

Hrishi and Manish exchanged a quick glance. There was no mistaking the surprised look on their faces.

"What's this about boss?" asked Hrishi.

"As you're aware, we were all from the same area Sir. Priya and I know each other right since our time at college."

"But you studied in two different colleges, didn't you?"

"The campuses were next to each other and we used to catch our return bus from the same stop. We used to meet everyday and somewhere down the line we..."

"Wasn't Nilesh aware of this?"

"No Sir. He was in Kolhapur from 9th Standard to graduation. He returned just after graduation to do his articleship."

"And you did it together, hmm. What happened then? Why didn't you go ahead?"

"She wasn't interested in taking it further Sir. She never was. The mistake was mine. Frankly we broke off, in the sense that Priya started avoiding me."

"I see. So what happened then?"

"Nilesh cleared CA quickly Sir, it took him just three attempts, so he was a CA by 22. His parents and Priya's knew each other well. So it was all arranged."

"I see. So how did you guys become partner? Wasn't that a factor?"

"Sir he was my friend. I might have had feelings for Priya, but he was unaware of it. If he moved ahead in life and did well for himself, I was glad for him. He never meant me any ill, nor did I. In any case, it was a sound business decision. I might have had some feelings for Priya, but that was long ago. I couldn't let that factor dictate the rest of my life."

"I get it now. The old flame never completely died out. It finally reached a point where it all boiled over and you decided to get rid of Nilesh."

"No Sir," said Pravin, almost quivering in fear. "I swear by God I have nothing to do with the murder."

"Hmm. So what happened when Nehal came back into his life?"

"Sir like I told you, I only suspected that something was amiss initially. I had no specific idea what was happening until one day I got a call from Priya to tell me that she suspected Nilesh was cheating on her. she wanted to know if I knew anything."

"I see. So what did you do then?"

"I told her that I had no idea. I only suspected that Nilesh was doing something behind our backs, but I had no idea what it had been until then. I wasn't even sure that he was seeing someone, much less who it was."

"I see. "So what happened on 24th July Pravin?"

"I don't know Sir. Nilesh told me that he was going to Kanheda. To be honest, that's when I first suspected that he was off to see Nehal, because he had once mentioned in the passing that she was in Kanheda. I had forgotten about it until he told me about this 'reunion'. I put two and two together and guessed what was happening."

"I see."

"The rest of it you know. The things I told you about our exchanges that night are all true."

"So what were you doing in Kanheda on the 26th?"

"Huh?" said Pravin, evidently surprised.

60

"I know you were there on the 26th so no point trying to hide anything. Just tell me what you were doing there," said Hrishi. It was pure bluff.

"Sir Priya requested me to find out what happened. We hadn't heard from Nilesh since 24th morning. I figured that he might be with Nehal, so I called up her company. Nilesh had told me that she worked for Diamond Cement. The person there told me that she had not reported to work, so I took down her residential address under a plausible pretext and went there. But she was not at home. I enquired with the neighbours. None of them had seen Nehal since a day or two. My subsequent attempts to get in touch with her and Nilesh were unsuccessful."

"Ah!" exclaimed Manish. So Pravin was indeed the unknown man who had gone enquiring about Nehal.

"I see. What do you plan to do now?"

"About what Sir?"

"About Priya? What do you intend?"

"Nothing Sir. I'm married with two kids. There's no chance."

"What about the insurance?"

"The insurance?"

"Yes, Nilesh's life insurance policy. What about it?"

"I don't know Sir."

"Are you sure?" asked Hrishi, hoping that Pravin would blurt out something in panic.

"I'm honest Sir," replied Pravin, "I have no idea about Nilesh's insurance."

"Hmm. Anything else you want to ask Manish?" asked Hrishi. Manish shook his head.

An Honest Confession

Hrishi and Manish stepped into the restaurant and took the seat just behind the cash counter. Most of the seats in the restaurant were now unoccupied as it was rather late in the afternoon. Hrishi quickly dialled Asha's number. She disconnected almost immediately, which she normally did only when she was somewhere close.

Sure enough, Asha turned up in a minute or two.

"So how was your meeting with Priya Karhadkar?"

"Interesting Sir, but not much that's new."

"Tell me about it."

"Sir I confronted her with the name of Nehal Patel. At first she tried to evade the question, but finally admitted that she suspected her husband of having an affair. She had no idea who the other woman was, but she had no doubt he was having an affair. She had no idea who Nehal Patel was."

"And why did she conceal this fact earlier."

"In her own words: 'do you expect me to go about telling an outsider that my husband is going around with another woman?'. I pointed out that we were the police. She told me that we could put her behind bars for it, but she would still have no regrets."

"I see. When did the affair start?"

"Sometime at the end of last year. She started suspecting it around December. Apparently Nilesh denied it completely."

"I see. What about her and Pravin?"

"She says that they were and they remain good friends. Apparently Pravin once asked her if she was interested, but she wasn't. Her marriage to Nilesh was an arranged one- not entirely with her consent by the way. It was just a coincidence that Nilesh and Pravin happened to be good friends."

"What about Nilesh? Was he aware of it?"

"No Sir. Apparently he wasn't in Pune during their college days. He didn't know about it and she never told him."

"That's strange. I mean, my wife and I, we share pretty much every little thing," said Hrishi. "If she didn't share something so important with Nilesh, that too about someone so close to the family, it means something isn't quite right."

"I asked her the same question Sir. Priya told me that she and Nilesh were never too close. He apparently conveyed a very different image before the world from what he really was. She says that pretty much everything he claimed to be before marriage was fake."

"I see. So she persisted with an unhappy marriage. Hmm... what about the insurance policy?"

"She confirmed it Sir. Priya made no effort to deny the fact that Nilesh was insured for eighty lakhs and that she had every intention to file a claim. She even added, for emphasis, that it was the least that was due to her after living seven years with that fellow."

"She said that?"

"Quite emphatically."

"So Nilesh didn't didn't exactly endear himself to his wife either...strange man!"

"I can't help sympathising with her Sir. Frankly, I can't help wondering why we're losing our time investigating this man's murder."

"We can't get emotional about it Asha. The fact is that a heinous crime has been committed. Its not our job to judge whether the case deserves to be investigated or not. Going by that logic, anyone would go about justifying murder by tainting the character of the victim. Besides, if we let the killer get away with it, he might feel emboldened to kill other innocent victims."

"You're right Sir."

"What's your general take on Priya?"

"The impression I got is that she's speaking the truth Sir."

"Either that, or she's a consummate actress," said Hrishi.

"Well Sir, I've been in the force since twelve years now. I've interacted with all kinds of people. My experience tells me that this woman is speaking the truth."

"Well, I'll take your word for it Asha. For now, let's proceed assuming that Priya has nothing to do with the murder, unless we get some information to the contrary."

"What about Pravin Sir?"

"Doesn't look likely to me Asha. That fellow looks too much of a coward to me. Besides, what he said pretty much tallies with what we've learnt from other sources."

"Incidentally," said Manish, speaking for the first time, "Pravin was that unknown fellow who went to Kanheda inquiring about Nehal."

"I see," said Asha. "But tell me Sir, if we're to accept that neither Pravin nor Priya are in any way involved, we've lost two suspects right away."

Hrishi nodded. "That pretty much means this case boils down to Nehal Patel and this big bearded fellow, whoever he is. The answer to this riddle lies with those two."

Two days later, Hrishi was in the field when his mobile rang. It was Manish's call. "Yes Manish?" said Hrishi, pressing the green button.

"Sir, we manage to trace down Nehal Patel's mobile phone. If you remember, I'd told you that it had been activated again."

"Oh yes Manish. Did you get any more information on it?"

"Yes Sir. We manage to trace it down to a chap called Abid Hassan in Punyaka. Through him we traced it down to a fence in that city. He didn't know the guy who sold it, but..."

"...let me guess, it was that big, *daadhiwala*. Am I right?"

"Yes Sir. The same chap. Just on a hunch I checked out and sure enough, we even found Nilesh's mobile there. It was sold to him by the same *daadhiwala*."

"Were you able to find out who this fellow was?"

"No Sir. As in Pritampur, that chap called him from a landline number. We traced it down to a PCO at Punyaka bus depot. We even went to the depot, but we weren't able to get any information on this *daadhiwala*."

"Great! Anything else?"

"That's about it Sir."

"In other words, we're no further."

"Yes Sir. Back to square one."

"Bloody... It feels like we're walking into a dark alley that has no end. *Bas ek baar yeh Nehal Patel apne haath mein aa jaye...*"

The Trail Goes Dead

It was a cool November evening. Hrishi was in DCP Patkar's cabin, discussing a case with his senior officer.

"Anything else Hrishi?" asked Shrikant.

"Nothing else Sir."

"Alright, great. Good work, as usual."

"Thank you Sir," said Hrishi, getting up to leave.

"One more thing Hrishi. What about that murder case in Kanheda? I remember transfering it to you. Haven't heard about it since two-three months now."

"That case fizzled out Sir. As you're aware, we got nothing concrete against the victim's partner or his wife. The case boils down to this other lady and this big bearded fellow who was with her. We haven't been able to establish that man's identity and this lady has completely disappeared. We never managed to trace either of them."

"You mean to say that she just disappeared into thin air?"

"Yes Sir. We checked out every possible avenue. There was no rail or air booking under that name either on 24th July or after."

"Which means she must have gone by road."

"So it seems Sir, but her car was still parked outside her house. We haven't been able to find out which car she used."

"Didn't you check with any of the toll nakas on the way?"

"We did Sir, but no one remembered seeing her."

"I see... well I guess that a dead end. Too bad. Anyway, you guys did a fantastic job of taking the case that far, considering you only had a photograph to work with when you started."

"Thank you Sir. I fear its one of *those* cases- the ones which just go dead. I'm afraid this will go down in our records as an unsolved crime," said Hrishi.

A Skeleton

It was a cold January morning. Constable Mahesh Hoskote was seated at his desk in Subhash Nagar police station in Kanheda. He was in convesation with the *chaiwallah* when the telephone instrument on his table started ringing.

"Hello?" said he, picking up the receiver.

"Hello? Subhash Nagar police station?"

"Yes. Constable Hoskote here."

"Sir my men have found a body," said the other man, evidently agitated.

"Okay, who are you? Where are you and where did you find the body?"

"Sir I'm Satish Chaudhary. I'm a contractor. We're building this road at Subhash Nagar Extension."

"Are you still there?"

"Yes Sir."

"Then stay there. I'm coming."

———✦———

SHO Shankar Prakash entered Dr. Narendra Gupta's room. "Good evening doctor," said he, greeting the forensic doctor. "*Kya halchal*?"

"Good evening Prakashji. *Sab badhiya.* Going well I hope."

"Ya sure, except for the weather. Unusually cold this year. Anyway, we'll come to that later doctor saahab. I came here for the report. I believe you completed your examination of that skeleton that was found in Subhash Nagar extension," said Prakash.

"Yes boss. I haven't completed the report. You'll have it by tomorrow afternoon."

"Okay. What did you find though?"

"Boss, the skeleton was of a woman. Judging by the development of the bones, she should have been around thirty-five when she died."

"How long has she been dead Sir?"

"Hard to say Prakashji. But considering the stage of decomposition and the nature of the soil in the place where the skeleton was found, it should be anywhere between 6 to 8 months."

"6 to 8 months? That means sometime between last May and July."

"Yes boss, sometime between May and July last year."

"Is it a case of murder?" asked Prakash. It almost certainly was. He was only seeking confirmation. As expected, Dr. Gupta nodded in affirmation. "What's the cause of death?"

"Suffocation. The condition of the cervical vertebrae suggests that she was either hanged or quite brutally strangled. I should think its a case of strangling rather than hanging."

"That is itself a lot Sir. So we're looking at a murder by strangulation. Hmm. What did you say the age was?"

"Over 30 but less than 35. The lady should have been in her early to mid 30s."

"What's the height of this lady?"

"She should have been 5'3" or 5'4"."

"I see. Thank you Sir. I'll initiate the search."

Manish's mobile started ringing. He hastily pulled the instrument out of his pocket. The call was from a landline number somewhere in Kanheda. Who on earth could it be? He took the call.

"Hello, am I speaking to Inspector Manish Deshpande?"

"Yes, speaking."

"Hello Deshpande Saahab, I'm SHO Shankar Prakash from Subhash Nagar police station in Kanheda."

"Oh, Prakashji. How're you sir? *Kaise yaad kiya*?"

"I'm good Deshpande saahab. Are you still with Crime Branch."

"Yes, very much so. Why?"

"Deshpande Saahab, we found the skeleton of an unidentified woman. Its of a woman in her early 30s who was around 5'3". I was going through the list of missing ladies and I found that lady you were searching for when you came to my police station last August."

"Okay!"

"I'm not sure about it, but it just occured to me that it could be her. I suggest you look out for it."

"Sure Prakash Saahab. Thanks a million."

———❖———

Manish knocked the door of Hrishi's cabin, where he was ushered in immediately.

"So tell me boss, what's up?" asked Hrishi, after they had completed the pleasantries.

"Sir remember that Kanheda murder case?"

"How could I ever forget it? After making you run around the state, we got nothing out of it."

"Sir there could be a new lead. Not sure yet."

"Okay, what's up?"

"Sir a road contractor found a skeleton which is still unidentified. They were extending an existing road, when they found this skeleton.

70

Its of a woman of in her mid 30s. Apparently she was strangled to death about six to eight months ago."

"Okay."

"Sir 6-8 months would mean sometime between last May and July. The list of missing women reported in Kanheda during that period includes Nehal Patel."

"Nehal Patel!" exclaimed Hrishi. "You mean..."

"It could be Sir. I don't know for sure, but it could be her."

"What if it is... hey, wait a minute, we can find out for sure if its her."

"How Sir?"

"Simple boss. Remember, you said that one of the people she called was her dentist?"

"Yes Sir. Ah, you mean..."

"Yes boss. Get her dental records. We can match the x-rays with the skull."

"I'll arrange for it Sir."

It was a cold evening, when Manish found himself in Hrishi's cabin. The later had just returned from a pretty tiring day in the field and looked visibly exhausted.

"So tell me Manish, what's it about?" asked Hrishi. They had just got over the usual pleasantries.

"Sir I did like you suggested. Its confirmed that the skeleton they found in Kanheda was indeed of Nehal Patel."

"I see. That means all our assumptions so far go flying out of the window."

"Yes Sir. According to the autopsy, she's been dead since six to eight months."

"We could put a more accurate date to it boss. By the look of things, she must have been murdered the same night as Nilesh."

"Yes Sir. It looks like she was murdered the same day and her mobile was switched off by the murderer. I spoke to SHO Shankar Prakash in Kanheda. I realised that the neighbour, whose testimony we got, never really saw Nehal go out that night. She told us that she saw her car going out. But she didn't see Nehal going out or coming back. She only saw that daadhiwala step out to open the gate."

"My God! That just shows how dangerous it is to make assumptions my dear fellow. We were so sure that Nehal was at the bottom of it, that we looked at the facts through that prism. You see boss, everything makes sense now. That fellow took out the car to get rid of the body, which is why he drove down a road which led nowhere," said Hrishi.

"But why did he bring the car back Sir?"

"That's the tricky part boss. Let's try and reconstruct what must have happened that night, assuming that there were two guys in the car which splashed Nehal's neighbour. One of them followed Nilesh and most probably, he was the one who murdered him."

"Right Sir. The other fellow, that daadhiwala murdered Nehal and then disposed off her body."

"Looks like it. He didn't have a car of his own, so he used Nehal's car."

"That means one of two things Sir. He must have taken an auto or taxi, which is unlikely since its a pretty isolated area. The other possibility, which is most likely, is that the other fellow came back to pick him up."

"Yes boss. It all fits in. That's the way it must have panned out. They had no choice but to leave Nehal's car. So the daadhiwala sells both mobile phones and the car, both of which were reasonably expensive. Its obvious that the plunder is incidental to the murder."

"Looks like it Sir. But that daadhiwala doesn't seem to have been present when Nilesh was killed, eventhough he had the car as well as the mobile. He must be the leader of the pack."

"Maybe, but its also possible that he was only helping out the other fellow and the plunder was an addition to his pay. You never know," said Hrishi. "Anyway, the question now is, whether those fellows were connected to Nilesh or to Nehal."

"I didn't get you Sir."

"We have been investigating so far on the assumption that the murderer was after Nilesh. In the light of what we've just discovered, there's every possibility that it was related to Nehal. Perhaps it was a jealous lover- maybe some friend or colleague who might have acted in jealousy."

"We checked out that angle Sir. If you remember, we got a report from Mumbai police. There was no reason to suspect her ex-husband and we didn't get any information on a possible boyfriend."

"In that case, we can assume that this daadhiwala and whoever else was with him knew Nilesh at a professional level, because we haven't got anything concrete on his family or his business partner."

"Looks like it Sir, but one thing I don't understand in that case. If they were after Nilesh, why did they kill Nehal?"

"They might have feared that Nilesh might have told her about them. Another possibility which just occured to me is that they did it to mislead us. If that was the idea, they pretty much succeeded. We've been chasing Nehal all along and what did we get? A dead end. We'd even written off this case. Had it not been for the accidental discovery of that skeleton, the case might have been forgotten by now."

"True Sir."

"This one's gone too far Manish, and I'm more responsible than anyone else for it. I should have involved myself more. Let's get cracking on this boss. We'll check out the people Nilesh interacted with in his professional capacity. *Sabka chittha nikal.*"

"Sure Sir."

"And get me everyone's call records. I'll look into it myself."

"Sure Sir."

A Fresh Lead

Manish stepped into the cabin of Hrishi, who had just called him. "Yes Sir?" asked he, taking his seat opposite his senior officer.

"Manish yaar, I browsed through the call records of Nilesh Karhadkar. There's this one number we seem to have overlooked. Look here," said Hrishi pointing out a number. "This is the last number he spoke to. Did you trace it?"

Manish took a quick look. "Yes Sir. You remember, I told you that number is of some chap with an unusual name? I thought I should trace it, but we got stuck with Nehal. I guess I lost sight of it," said Manish sheepishly.

"Its okay boss. With your workload, I can understand that you got stuck with other cases. We made the mistake of assuming that Nehal was at the bottom of this. Anyway, *jo hua so hua*. We can't change what's gone. Let's look ahead," said Hrishi. Manish nodded, relieved that his senior officer was not making a fuss of what was a clear omission on his part.

"I tried calling this number. Its out of service."

"It was already out of service then Sir. I remember dialing it."

"Trace down this number ASAP boss. Get all the details you can. For all you care, this one could be that *daadhiwala*."

"Sure Sir."

Hrishi entered Sukh Sagar restaurant. Looking around, he spotted Manish seated at a table on the right hand corner at the far end of the room. He walked over to the table.

"Good evening Sir."

"Good evening Manish. Placed the order?"

"Yes Sir. Your *chai-samose* should be arriving."

"Great. been another long day. I guess it must have been the same for you. Anyway, let's get down to business. What did you get boss?"

"Sir that number was activated on 24th July last year and it was also switched off that night. it was never used any time before or since"

"I see! Who was it?"

"Someone called Shijo Alexander Sir. That number was used to make only one call. I have asked for all available details, including the vendor who sold this connection. We should be receiving all the information in a day or two."

"Alright, good work Manish. We're getting there for sure. This Shijo is almost certainly the one we're looking for."

Hrishi walked into Praful General Stores, accompanied by Manish. "Ji saahab?" asked the man at the counter. "I want to see the owner of this store," said Hrishi in Hindi.

"I'm the owner Sir. Tell me."

"I'm ACP Bharadwaj from Madhavgadh Crime Branch. I want to inquire about a mobile connection that was sold by you."

"Okay Sir. do you have the details?"

"Yes, its in this piece of paper. I want a copy of all the documents this fellow submitted. This connection was sold last July."

"Yes Sir, just a minute," said the owner. He took a look at the paper and asked his assistant to bring the 'puranawalla' file, which was brought presently.

"There you are Sir," said the man, pointing out the documents related to that connection.

"The photograph on the PAN card isn't clear. And where are the other documents?"

"Sir I don't have them..."

"Why? How do you think we're going to get that fellow's address? And did you at least check the originals."

"Ji Sir."

"You're lying boss. Its obvious that you didn't check anything. You've just issued the connection without proper documentation. Did the guy who took this connection come here personally?"

"I don't remember Sir."

"Take your mind back in time and remember boss. This is a murder investigation."

"Ab Sir, we issue thousands of connection... wait, I think I remember this one. It should be that tall, hefty fellow. That pen I gave him was of bad quality, he smudged some of the ink because of the way he wrote, look here"

"Oh yes. Did that fellow have a beard?"

"Yes Sir, you're right. That fellow had a beard. He took this connection some months ago."

"And is this photograph is his?"

The shopkeeper took a look at the passport size photograph that was attached with the application form. He shook his head. "No Sir, its not him for sure."

"Do you remember that fellow? Can you help our artist make a sketch?"

"Sorry Sir, but its been too long. I'll recognise him if I saw him, but I don't remember enough to make a sketch. I remembered that fellow because of his size," said the shopkeeper.

"Okay, fine," said Hrishi. "If you remember anything else, let us know. And consider yourself lucky that you got away with this."

"Sir what do I do? If I refuse to give the connection, there are ten others who are ready to give."

"Do you even know who the other person is? Had that fellow been a terrorist you would have been in big trouble now. Let the money go boss, its better to lose some business than find yourself in jail."

"Sorry Sir."

"If you continue doing this boss, someday you'll genuinely be. *Chal*," said Hrishi, gesturing to Manish.

"Our mystery man seems to be everywhere," said Manish. "But how do we trace him now?"

"Simple boss. Either he's Shijo, or Shijo will lead us to him," said Hrishi.

"I didn't get you Sir."

"Look at the address in the application form."

"Its in Shilahar!" exclaimed Manish.

"Exactly. We know that it wasn't one of his friends or family members who got rid of Nilesh. Obviously it was someone who had a professional connection with him. the key to this mystery is in Shilahar."

Following the Trail

Manish was at the wheel, with Hrishi seated next to him. "There's the house boss," said the later, pointing to the third house to the left.

They parked the vehicle and entered the gates. Moving ahead, Hrishi rang the bell. The door was opened by a young man in his mid 20s. "Yes?" he asked.

"I'm ACP Bharadwaj from Madhavgadh Crime Branch. I want to see Shijo Alexander."

"Shijo? He no longer lives here Sir."

"Where's he now?"

"I'm not sure Sir. He was the previous occupant so I never met him, but you can check out with the estate agent who rented him this apartment."

"Get me his mobile number."

"Sure Sir."

A few minutes later, Hrishi and Manish were back outside, standing by the car. Hrishi had the mobile instrument to his ear. He had just dialled the number the young man had given him. Presently the call was answered.

"Hello, am I speaking to Kalpesh Sawant?" asked Hrishi in Hindi.

"Yes Sir, Kalpesh Sawant here," came the reply in Hindi.

"Hello Mr. Sawant, I'm ACP Bharadwaj from Madhavgadh Crime Branch. We're looking for a man called Shijo Alexander. I understand you had fixed him a house at Shastri Nagar."

"Shastri Nagar....oh yes, that mallu boy. Yes Sir, I remember him."

"Good, where is he now?"

"I don't know Sir. He left last year. I met him just once or twice. You can find out from his office, though. Someone there should be able to tell you."

"Where's it?"

"I'm not sure Sir, but I have the office number. One of the guys who work there gave Shijo my reference."

"Give me the number," said Hrishi.

Hrishi dialled the number that Sawant had given him. the moment he heard the welcome message, he disconnected. "That name..." said he, clearly trying to recollect something.

"What's it Sir?"

"There was a welcome message. Its a company called Dixons Chemicals. Where have I heard that... oh yes, oh yes! That's the one. I know where it is. Let's go."

⊰❖⊱

About half an hour later, Hrishi and Manish entered the office of Dixons Chemicals, where Hrishi asked for Ashish Goyal. They were ushered into his cabin immediately.

"Hello officer, what brings you here Sir? Still investigating Nilesh's murder?" asked Ashish, visibly surprised to see them.

Hrishi nodded. "Its been a complicated case Goyal saahab, but I believe we're somewhere close to solving it."

"Great! Can I help you in any way?"

"Yes Mr. Goyal. We're looking for a man called Shijo. I understand he works here."

"Shijo Alexander?" asked Ashish. Hrishi nodded. "Yes Sir, that fellow used to work here, but it must be a year since he left. What's he got to do with this case?"

"He's one of the last few people who spoke to Nilesh."

"Shijo? Not possible Sir! He was a marketing guy. I'm not sure he ever met the auditors."

"Maybe, maybe not. Leave that to us to figure that out Mr. Ashish."

"Sir Shijo is no longer in India. He's been in Qatar since close to a year now. He got a job there with some real estate company and left."

"Did he?"

"Yes Sir, Shijo hasn't been in India since a year now."

"Goyal Saahab, even we suspect that someone has just used his name. But the person who took the connection not only used his name, but even used a copy of his PAN card."

"His PAN card?"

Hrishi nodded. "Since that person used Shijo's local address here, I suspect that its someone in your company. Who would be in a position to get his passport size photos and pan card copy?"

"That would be in his employee file Sir."

"How many people have access to it?"

"Well Sir, myself and all the heads of department. So there's the head of finance, HR & admin, IT, marketing and purchases, apart from Raghu and Sheetal in HR & Admin, so that makes it eight of us."

"That's all? You have only five departments?"

"Yes Sir. We're not such a huge company. We don't need too many departments."

"So there are in all 8 people who can access the records. Hmm..."

"Is any of them a tall, hefty fellow with a beard?" asked Manish.

"Tall, hefty and bearded? My God!"

"So there is someone like that."

"Yes Sir, there's Mohammed Rafique, our head of finance."

"Mohammed Rafique? Of course, that hefty chap I met last time. But he was clean shaven."

"He used to have a small beard Sir. He took it off some months ago."

"Shit! It was all there, right in front of us. We failed to see it. Call him here immediately."

"He's not here Sir. I mean, he's gone out on some personal work."

"Personal work? What personal work?"

"I don't know Sir. He just told me that he was out on some personal work and that he would be back by afternoon."

"Do you know where he would be?"

"I don't know Sir. Shall I call him?"

"No Mr. Ashish. Whatever you do, don't call him. Give me his residential address."

"Sure Sir, just a minute," said Ashish. He hastily walked to the computer and started typing something. In a moment he started jotting down something on a piece of paper. "There Sir, here's his address."

"Manish, stay right here. I'm going to the police station. If that guy turns up, just arrest him. I'll leave Govind here with you."

"Sure Sir."

"Ashish saahab, thank you very much for your help. We may have to trouble you again."

"Anytime Sir. I'll do anything I can to help you."

On the Threshold of Success

H rishi dialled Manish's number. It was around half past six in the evening. Manish took the call immediately.

"Hello Manish, did he turn up?"

"No Sir. If he had, I would have surely called you."

"Did he call up anytime?"

"No Sir. I've been with Mr. Ashish most of the time. There was no call from Rafique."

"As I thought. He didn't come here either and I don't think he's going to."

"Why Sir?"

"He wouldn't have taken so long boss. Do you know that his mobile has been switched off?"

"Switched off?"

"Yes boss. That fellow switched off his instrument several hours ago. Its inconceivable that he didn't have the opportunity to charge it yet. He's obviously turned it off, so that we can't track him."

"But Sir..."

"Is there anyone in front of you?"

"No Sir. I'm in Ashish's cabin, he's not here right now."

"Alright. Be careful what you say as long as you're there."

"Don't worry Sir. There's no one here. But Sir, if that fellow ran away, its obvious that someone informed him about us."

"Yes boss, no doubt about it. So Rafique wasn't in this alone. There was someone else with him and in all probability, that someone else is the one who killed Nilesh."

"What do we do now?"

"Nothing. I'll have the office and Rafique's house watched with the help of the local police, though I suspect he isn't going to turn up anytime soon. We'll have to find him, wherever he is. In the meanwhile, let's start building our case."

"Okay...," said Manish.

"We know who our person is boss and we are going to get him eventually, but our efforts will come to nought if we can't collect the evidence needed for a conviction. Get a photograph of Rafique and show it to all the people who saw that big, bearded person.We'll need witnesses."

"Yes Sir."

"And speak to the people there. Get as much information about Rafique as possible. In the meanwhile, I'll speak to Shilahar Police. *Us company ka pura chittha nikalte hain.* The answer to this riddle lies somewhere there."

Loose Ends Tie Up

Manish was seated in Hrishi's cabin. It was three days since they had been to Shilahar.

"We've got an update from Shilahar police. Their informers seem to be quite effective boss," said Hrishi.

Manish was about to say something when Hrishi's mobile started ringing. "Hello Bangera saahab. Good morning."

"Good morning officer. Is it a good time to talk?" came the voice of Hiren Bangera, with the sing-song accent typical of south Indians.

"Sure is. I've been waiting for your feedback."

"The good news is, I've managed to take a look at the accounts. *Solid jhol hai officer.*"

"How so?"

"There are many points officer. Let me try and explain in simple terms. To begin with, their purchases are eating up a huge chunk of their revenues, a lot more than you would normally expect for a company in the chemical industry. I suspect the bills are inflated or some of the stuff has been siphoned off and sold, possible both. I hope I'm not sounding too technical."

"Not at all. I understand Sir, I've done my BCom so I have some understanding of these things."

"Okay! Now there's another thing that's pretty wierd officer. Their receivables, I mean the money they have to receive from the buyers of the company's goods is incredibly high. Almost half the money they should be receiving from the sales is still to be received."

"What does it signify Sir?"

"There could be many reasons. Possibly they are lazy about getting back their money, which is quite unlikely. They don't have a big stock of finished goods at the end of the year, which means that the stuff they've produced has indeed been sold. I suspect they're collecting the money, but not accounting for it."

"You mean to say that the money to be received has actually been received and siphoned off elsewhere, but in their accounts, its still being shown as receivable."

"That's right officer. That's exactly what seems to be the case. If I could take a look at the accounts, I'd get a clearer picture. This is what I gather from the balance sheet and profit & loss account. Let's say its like judging a movie by its trailer."

"Okay. I understand Sir. Tell me one thing, will the auditor be aware of it?"

"Has to be officer. Its just a 70 odd crore company and its owned by just two people- what we'd call a closely held company. The accounts of this kind of company shouldn't be too complicated. Any CA worth his salt will be able to say in just a preliminary glance that there's something seriously wrong there and I can say with confidence that its been going on since at least three years now. There's no way they could have done it for so long without the auditor knowing about it."

"So you mean to say that the auditor was involved in the scheme."

"I should think so officer. There's another thing I may add, for all that it is worth."

"What's that Sir?"

"Someone very senior in the company should be involved in this."

"Its the head of finance Sir. He's the one we're collecting evidence against. That's why DCP Patkar troubled you."

"The head of finance may be involved officer, but he can't be the only one."

"You think so?"

"I'm sure. You see, the finance guy only signs the cheques and approves the payments. Its quite difficult to pull off a fraud without his help or knowledge, but its also impossible for the finance guy to do it himself."

"I see. To be honest Sir, we suspect that one of the other GMs is also involved in this."

"I should think someone still higher should be involved officer. In a closely held company, normally the owners reserve the authority to approve even the smallest transaction. In any case, the company's overdraft has gone up from six odd lakhs two years ago to over forty lakhs now, which cannot possibly happen without the knowledge of the owners in such a company."

"Is it possible for employees to do it?"

"Only if the owner has no understanding of accounting. But in that case, the employees should be in a position to authorise transactions, which is rare in such companies."

"Okay. Just one last question Sir. Is it possible to find out if there are any employees who can authorise transactions, without the *companyvale* knowing about it?"

"Generally, no. But there is one possibility. Contact the banks where they have their accounts and find out who are authorised to sign the company's cheques. That should give you a fairly good idea."

"Alright, thank you very much Sir. You've been a great help."

"My pleasure officer. Bye."

"What was that about Sir?" asked Manish.

"DCP Patkar's idea yaar. He asked a CA to get us inside information on Dixons Chemicals. What he's saying tallies with the information we got from the local sources there. Someone is siphoning money from that company."

"That's Rafique Sir. He was the head of finance. Who better?"

"The CA is saying that he couldn't have done it alone, which further confirms what we suspected boss. There is someone else in that office who is with Rafique in this racket."

"If things go to plan, I might be able to tell you by the end of the day who it is."

Hrishi raised his eyebrows. "How So?"

"Sir, as you're aware, I was in Ashish Goyal's cabin when we were speaking the other day," said Manish. Hrishi nodded. "As it happened, there was a group photo on the wall behind his desk, here look."

"Okay, so you captured it?"

"Yes Sir. It just occured to me that other person, whoever he is, also went to Kanheda with Rafique. If that other person is in this photo, which is likely, someone or the other might have seen him too."

"Yes, you're right! Superb thinking Manish."

"Thank you Sir. I'm leaving for Kanheda now, which is why I said that I might be in a position to confirm by today evening who the other person is. Incidentally, that fence Bandya as well as the shopkeeper in Pritampur who sold the prepaid connection recognised Mohammed Rafique immediately. Hopefully we'll get some more witnesses in Kanheda today."

"God willing. My only fear right now, is that we still don't have a motive. They may be a fraud going on and Nilesh might have cooperated with whoever is doing it. But then why would he want to get rid of the person who's on his side?"

"No idea Sir. That's something which still beats me."

"Anyway, hopefully we should soon have the answers. Nonetheless, great work Manish. All the best for today."

"Thank you Sir."

Coup de Grace

Hrishi and Manish stepped into the office of Dixon Chemicals, accompanied by constable Govind Mane. They were immediately ushered into the cabin of Ashish Goyal.

"Hello officer," said Ashish Goyal. "Welcome once again. Would you like to have some chai- coffee?"

"No thank you," said Hrishi. "We won't need it."

"As you like it Sir. Were you able to trace Rafique? He's neither come here nor contacted us since the last time you came here. His mobile too has been switched off."

"No Mr. Goyal. We haven't found him yet. But no problem. You see, there was someone else in your company who was with him in all that. We've come to get him."

"Really! Who?"

"You."

"What? Are you..."

"Calm down, be seated. No point getting agitated now. We have witnesses who saw you in Kanheda that night. You might have escaped identification Mr. Goyal, but giving a five hundred rupee note at the toll gate for a ticket that costs twenty is not the cleverest idea. There's of course, your phone records and there's Rafique's as well. He could testify against you."

"I'm sure there's a mistake Sir."

"Stop kidding me Mr. Goyal. We've checked out Rafique's phone records. There was a call from your number to his on the day we were here. We came at eleven and you called him twice that day, once at quarter past eleven from your mobile. You called him once again at half past seven from a PCO in Nagar Chowk. The man at the PCO recognised you. You had withdrawn twenty thousand from the ATM, which you most probably handed over to Rafique when you met him that evening at the Dhaba on NH 3. He switched on his mobile for a short while when he was in that area. We went there looking for him and the owner of the dhaba there identified both of you. So stop bullshiting and tell us the truth."

The look of surprise on Ashish Goyal's face had given way to fear. "I...never thought..." he started, searching for words.

"Your game is up Ashish Goyal. You made a pretty good job of throwing us off the track, from the entire plan down to identifying Rafique the other day. You figured that we would identify him anyway, so you pretended to be helping us out. Isn't that so?"

"Yes Sir. I had no choice, so went along with you," said Ashish, barely able to speak coherently. He had the look of a broken man.

"Okay, tell us from the beginning Ashish. What's all this about? We know you did it, we also know how you did and there's ample proof of that. Now tell us why you did all this."

"Sir I've been siphoning the company money since some time now."

"We know that, when did it start?" asked Hrishi.

"I..." started Ashish, surprised once again. "I started about four years ago Sir."

"Why?"

"Sir Rajiv and I started this business nine years ago. He had the money and I had the brain and the enterprise to build it up. From just one and a half crores in the first year, we grew to over thirty crores after the fourth year of operation," said Goyal. He paused to have a glass of water.

89

"Okay, go on. I'm listening," said Hrishi.

Goyal smacked his by now parched lips. "Rajiv had started a second business in the the UAE, where he was manufacturing lubricants. Its a pretty good business Sir and it grew very fast. He started spending more and more time there. His involvement here was virtually zero. I was the one running the show here. So when we had a bumper profit four years ago, I felt that it was time I got my due. He took 60% of the profit, even though his contribution to running the business was zero..."

"Okay..."

"So one day, when he was here on a visit, we met up over dinner. I put forward the proposal to Rajiv. It wasn't as if I was kicking him out. I offered to buy out his share of the business. That way the business would be entirely mine and Rajiv would also get his money."

"And he refused, isn't it?"

"Yes Sir. I also proposed a change in the shareholding pattern, so that I got an equal share of the profits, but Rajiv refused even that offer. He argued that he was the one who had invested the bulk of the funds, so the profits too should go to him. He just refused to listen to my arguments."

"I see. So that's when you decided to defraud him."

"Yes Sir. *Ungli tedhi karni hi padi.* We started siphoning off the money received and I even started buying from select suppliers at very high rates, for which I got a cut. We were well established, selling was not a problem. On paper we were just making a small profit but the business was flourishing, and so was I."

"So that's why you changed the auditors. Am I right?"

"Yes Sir. Ironically, it was through Rajiv's contacts that we found Nilesh. I heard that he was the sort of auditor who would cooperate if we wanted to play around with the accounts. That kind of information is easily available in the market."

"And you couldn't do it without the help of the finance guy, so you also got your man on board, isn't it?"

"Yes Sir. It was purely by chance that the previous guy left the company. To be honest, there's when I saw my chance and Rafique was the perfect candidate. He loved shortcuts in life. He desperately wanted money, so he agreed to play ball."

"Okay! Pretty convenient arrangement. So why did you murder Nilesh? He was helping you, wasn't he?"

"He was helping me Sir, and I paid him handsomely for it, but that bloody fellow grew too greedy. He started asking for more. He always wanted a little extra, until it reached a point where I refused to give him any more."

"When did this happen?"

"Sometime last summer. I almost doubled what I was giving until then. That bloody fellow built a house in his native place using the money I gave him, but it was still not enough. He started threatening me that he would spill the beans before Rajiv."

"Oh I see, so he was blackmailing you."

"Yes Sir. Rafique started panicking. If the story got to the CA Institute, he could be stripped off his degree. So we started keeping an eye on Nilesh. We discovered that he was having an affair with another lady in Kanheda. I threatened to reveal it to his wife. That bloody fellow was so shameless, he laughed at us. He asked me to go and tell his wife directly. He'd be only too happy if she walked out on him."

"He said that?"

"Yes Sir. That left us no option but to get rid of him. He was too greedy and there was going to be no end to his blackmail unless we acted first. So we planned it out."

"Okay. Tell us about it. What exactly happened that night? Remember, we know most of the details, so we can easily catch you if you try to give us a cock and bull story."

"Nilesh was in Kanheda and we knew that he would most probably leave on 24th July, because he was to come to our office on the 25th. We figured that it would be the best time to get rid of him. No one would even remotely suspect us and all the suspicion would fall on Nehal Patel. We knew that our mobile location might get us caught, so it was essential to get a new connection which no one should be able to trace back to us. Rafique said that he could do it. That's where I made a mistake. I should have checked what he was doing. That stupid fellow..."

"You're digressing Ashish. Get back to the story."

"Well, alright. So Rafique got us new connections and new, cheap instruments. Rafique also arranged for a car from a garage wallah he knows in his area. With that, we were ready to swing into action. We went to Kanheda on 24th afternoon and waited for him there. That fellow left around seven. As planned, I followed him, leaving behind Rafique to take care of Nehal Patel."

"Why did you have her murdered? She wasn't involved in this."

"To throw the police off the trail. Just in case the police identified Nilesh and started investigating his murder, they should be under the impression that Nehal Patel was the perpetrator. If she were to disappear completely, it would look all the more convincing."

"Okay. Carry on."

"So Rafique strangled her and then took the body away in Nehal's car. He buried the body in a place where we figured no one would ever go. In the meanwhile, I followed Nilesh until he went past city limits to the highway, where no one would see us."

"How did you do it? You were going in your car and he in his. How did you manage to handle both cars?"

"Sir I called up Nilesh, changing my voice. I told him that I had something very important to tell him. With the changed voice and the unknown number, that fellow never even vaguely suspected that it could be me. I asked him to wait at a dhaba on the highway, where I would be coming in a silver grey Esteem."

"And he did like you said?"

"Yes Sir. I stopped the car there and he hopped in."

"Wasn't he surprised to see you?"

"He was Sir, but he didn't suspect anything. He just got in. So we started talking and we got into an argument. It didn't matter, because my mind was made up. finally, I stopped the car at a bridge over the river. It was quite dark. It was the perfect time and place. I parked the car and we got off. That fellow never saw it coming. It was over in no time. There was no one around. I took anything with which he could be identified, including his shirt, since it was made to order."

"Oh! That's why his shirt was missing. That explains it."

"Yes Sir. Once I was satisfied that there was nothing left on his person with which he could be identified, I threw his body into the river."

"I see. So that was it as far as Nilesh was concerned. What did you do after that?"

"I drove back to Kanheda. Rafique had disposed off the body and parked Nehal's car. He was waiting for me there. From there, we drove down to the dhaba where Nilesh's car was still parked. Rafique got off and took Nilesh's car. I asked him to keep all the mobile phones with him and not switch them on any time."

"What about the car? What did you plan to do with it?"

"I asked Rafique to destroy the car completely, so that no one would ever know of it. That was my second mistake. That stupid fellow became greedy. Two expensive mobile phones and a Tata Safari in good shape was too much for him to resist."

"Too good to resist. He sold them off and that's how we got to him. Hmm, I must say you did a pretty good job of covering your traces. Very well planned Ashish. Anyway, where's Rafique?"

"He's gone Sir."

"Gone? Where?"

"Gone Sir. I got rid of him."

"My God! How?"

"I disposed him off when I went to meet him at the dhaba. That money I withdrew was not to pay Rafique, it was to pay Zafarbhai."

"Zafarbhai? Who's he?"

"He's a supariwallah Sir. I had to pay him two lakhs to get rid of Rafique. I was about fifteen thousand short, which is why I withdrew from the ATM."

"Okay, carry on."

"So Zafarbhai followed me in the car behind. After our meeting, Rafique came with me. I was supposed to drive him to the railway station in Pritampur. I stopped the car along the route at a pretty secluded spot. There Zafarbhai came in and did his bit."

"How did he kill Rafique?"

"He shot him Sir."

"Where's the body?"

"I don't know Sir. I asked him to dispose off the body. He knows where it is."

"Why did you have to get him? You already had practice in this kind of thing."

"You've seen Rafique Sir. How could I overpower him? Besides, getting rid of the body would have been another headache. I figured it would be much easier to get a professional."

"I see. Well, smart thinking Ashish, but you forgot that every little thing you do leaves a trail. No matter how hard you try to conceal it, its impossible to cover it up. You can supress the truth, but you cannot ever bury it. Anyway, get me this Zafarbhai's number. We'll trace that fellow down too. He can't escape us."

Conclusion

M anish entered Hrishi's cabin. The later looked up. "Hey
Manish! Come in boss, be seated. Sorry, I couldn't take your
call. Got stuck with a visitor."

"No problem Sir. The good news is, our mission is accomplished.
They've found Rafique's body. Fortunately, one bullet lodged in his
body and to add to it, they even recovered the *khatta* that Zafar used.
Its been sent for the ballistics report."

"Fantastic. Great job Manish. That rounds it up. Ashish and Zafar
have both confessed. That plus the body of Rafique and the ballistics
report will make a pretty strong chargesheet."

"Yes Sir. It sure will."

"The credit goes to you Manish. This would have never been
possible."

"Thank you Sir, but I think the credit goes to you too. We might
have never arrived at the truth if you hadn't taken over. That one
number cracked it."

"My dear fellow, we were both equally at fault. You see, the facts
were there right before us all along. Its just that we formed pre-
conceived notions and lazily looked at facts through that prism. We
first suspected Priya and Pravin. When we got to know of Nehal, the
suspicion shifted to her. At each stage, we looked at the facts purely
from the standpoint of their involvement."

"True Sir. But for the incredible good fortune of Nehal's body being found, this case would have been forgotten by now."

"That's the greatest challenge for an investigator Manish, seperating the red herrings from the real clues. If you manage it, you succeed. If not, you end up groping around in an endless dark alley."